Star City Publ

MW00916202

NATURE'S
QUEST

A Dangerous Entanglement

ANGEL WILLIAMS

Star City Publications

P.O Box 70384

Baltimore Maryland 21237

www.iamangelwilliams.com

Nature's Quest - A Dangerous Entanglement Copyright ♥ 2021 Angel Williams

ISBN- 13: ON FILE

ISBN- 10: ON FILE

First printing 2021

Printed in the United States of America

2 0 1 1 9 0 2 7 4 0

This is a work of fiction. Any references or similarities to actual events, real people, living, or dead, or to real locales are intended to give the novel a sense of reality. Any similarity in other names, characters, places, and incidents is entirely coincidental.

ACKNOWLEDGMENTS

Hello readers! I'm back at it again. First and foremost I want to give all praises and glory to God! I'm forever thanking God for my great talent, him blessing me with this give was a pure life saver. Writing keeps me together and it keeps me sane. Secondly I want to thank my beautiful mother Brenda Williams, she pushes me to my highest and she's done that since I was yay high, always pushing me and supporting me no matter what.

Thirdly my lovely daughters, miss Kaydence Miracle Marie better know as Kady Baby, Kay'Miyah Angela Dream and Kay'lani Diane Star. Thank God for blessing me with thie most amazing beautiful little girls, I no longer just write for myself or for my readers, I write for my girls. Paving their future, to the best of my capability.

To all my amazing family members that support me

thank you so much. Just to name a few my sisters Joy Williams. My brother James Williams Jr.

My aunts, Doris Patterson, Carolyn E. Tina F. a few of my cousins too many of you to mention. To my friends! Thank you all so much for being there and supporting me when I truly needed it. And to my lovely readers. Oh my, it's way too many of you to name. I have my A 1's since day one and I truly appreciate you all a bunches! You all mean the world to me, as a writer I'm growing daily and my fan base is raising through the roof, thanks to all of my supporters who has been devoutly sharing the word about me and my stories. Please continue to spread the word and let ALL of you friends know about me. I owe you all a million of thanks, hugs and kisses!

To all of my supporters and my loyalties. I'm forever grateful for you all. And I will never forget you, so please sign your name here

_____!

Special thanks to Michael Davis, who helped me create this story... And another special thank you to the entire Nature's Quest cast and crew. This story impacted a powerful insight on reality that so many of us live in, with the way the world is today. The movie, moved me so much that I had to tell the story. I'm more than grateful that I was blessed with amazing actors and crew to help pull this story off, I specially want to thank my two leads Chris Foxx Clanton SR and Lashay Smith for all the hard work and effort that was put into bringing these characters to life. For believing in my vision and executing it to perfection!

We can't help who we are... and we can't help who we love. Take a glimpse into this heart-wrenching love story. Nature has her battles that she chooses to defeat in her own way. She prayed for love and acceptance. After a brutal attack and almost losing her life, she decided to change her life completely and become the woman inside who she truly fell in love with.

Quest was a sucker for love. Mr. Lover Boy wore his heart on his sleeve. After countless failed relationships, he gave up on dating. That lasted until he started using a dating app, where he met someone he could love and live happily with for the rest of his life. After a year of online dating, the two finally met. Their love was unique yet fatal. After deception, a love web, and a bucket of lies, someone just may have a deadly price to pay...

CHAPTER ONE

*N*ature cautiously glanced around the empty hospital room. The only sound was the constant beeps of the medical devices. Her harsh tears and sniffles fell upon deaf ears.

"Ahhh-h-h-h! Why me? Why me?" Nature hollered, having a full-blown fit. She was already in so much pain, and she no longer cared about anything. Nearly to the point of no return, she grabbed her own hair and started yanking it until she had a handful of her tresses. Nature then began to slap herself across the face. "Why didn't you bastards kill me? Why-y-y-y-y?" she cried in a complete rage and state of self-hatred.

Out of breath and now feeling all the unnecessary pain that she put herself through, she sat in pure shock. The tears came even harder, and the self-inflicted injuries left even more bruises all over her already damaged face. She panted, trying to find her breath.

"Why did this happen to me?" Nature softly whispered. Hearing soft knocks on the door, she pushed her disheveled hair behind her ears. "Get yourself together right now, Nature," she told herself.

"Nature, it's me," Michelle cooed from the other side of the door.

Nature quickly wiped her eyes, removing any evidence that she had been shedding tears and beating herself up over a damn situation that she couldn't prevent.

"The door is unlocked. Come in," Nature softly spoke.

Michelle walked in. Her heels softly clicked against the floor as she made her way to Nature's bed.

Moving Nature's leg to the side, Michelle sat down beside her.

"I'm so thankful you are okay, Nature. When I got the call, all I could think about was losing you," Michelle admitted.

Nature turned her head, facing the window. Baltimore's skyline was so beautiful, especially from where she sat on the thirty-fourth floor of Mercy hospital.

"I'm so sorry! I didn't mean to scare you. It wasn't like I went and damn near got myself killed intentionally."

Nature's eyes rapidly blinked. She couldn't hold back the tears that were fighting to drop from her eyes. Her face was drenched with tears of sorrow as her mind went back to the vicious night that she was violently attacked. Her skin crawled with pain, veins pumped with a mixture of fear, hurt, and hatred. With all the mixed emotions bundled up inside of her, she let out a loud, heart-wrenching cry. So loud and painful that it caused Michelle to jump.

"I didn't deserve any of that. I didn't deserve any of that shit!" Nature screamed.

Michelle scooted closer to her friend and gently wrapped her arms around her.

"You are so right, baby girl. You didn't deserve any of the bullshit that happened to you," she agreed.

"I swear I am going to kill every one of them bastards! I remember their faces, and I promise I am going to slaughter them!" Nature stated through gritted teeth.

Her mind roamed back to that night. She shivered a bit as she replayed that night over and over in her head. Possibly for the thousandth time.

Earlier that day, Nature had promised herself to have the best day yet. As she stood in front of her floor-length mirror, dressing her face in MAC makeup, she vowed to release all the demons that were temporarily defeating her. She was going to let all bygones be bygones and nothing more. Nature was going to give herself the freedom she needed to live a life of prosperity and peace. Oh yes, peace was something she would no longer allow anyone to steal. Share, maybe, but never steal from her.

"Girl, get your shit together because this is your year, Nature!" She gave herself the quick pep talk that she would typi-

cally have. This daily routine was relatively fresh but rejuvenating to her soul and placed her spirits at the highest level.

"The goals: new car, new house, and new man. Manifest that shit right now!" She continued the self-motivation as she lined her lips with her pink lipstick and filled in the middle to perfection.

Nature smacked her lips together and stared at her gorgeous reflection in the mirror. She was a baddie for sure, and gorgeous as hell...

The pain, the expense, was worth every penny. It wasn't cheap to be a girl like herself. But again, she wasn't entirely responsible. The beauty maintenance fee was, of course, always at someone else's expense.

She pulled up her high waist cut-up jeans just above her belly button. Flicking her long tresses over her shoulder, she gazed at her plump ass in the mirror. Satisfied with her overall look, Nature grabbed her oversized Louie bag and marched down her steps.

Once she got in her car, she pulled out her cellphone to call Michelle. Not just her best friend but her only friend.

"What time will you be ready?" Nature questioned.

Michelle glanced down at her cell phone, checking the time. After partying like a rock star for three days in a row, she couldn't pull herself out of bed, even if she tried. Exhausted was an understatement. Not to mention, all the Mollys she popped and the white girl she sniffed was starting to take a toll on her body.

"Ummm, hmmm, I absolutely cannot. And I will not be coming out with you tonight, Nature. I can't keep up with you!

Honey, everything on my body hurts like hell from top to bottom. Hell, my toes even hurt!" Michelle exaggerated.

"Come on, Chelle Chelle! I want to go out. Look, I'll buy you your favorite seafood pasta from Mo's. Ohhh-h, I'll add a drink with it too," Nature begged.

"No can do, honey. No Sam, no ham, no ma'am." Michelle shook her head.

Nature sucked her teeth. "Whatever. I'm going out by myself then since you want to be a party pooper."

"Good, have fun. Have a drink or a few for me. And don't do anything that I won't do." Michelle laughed.

"And exactly what won't you do?" Natured giggled.

"Exactly! Good night, and I love you."

"Love you more," Nature replied and ended the call.

Those were facts. Nature and Michelle had a special love for each other and an extraordinary friendship that many couldn't understand. They shared so many deep, dark secrets that they would both take to the grave with them. No physical fights had ever occurred between the two of them. Maybe a simple disagreement here and there but nothing more.

Two hours later, Nature pulled up to the club. Seeing how thick the line was excited her. She quickly scanned the area, looking for a parking spot, and decided to park right beside an alley.

As soon as she got out of her car, Nature heard a bunch of footsteps. At that moment, something in her gut told her to run, but she decided that she was overthinking stuff, so she went ahead and popped her trunk to change her shoes. Nature glanced around and saw two guys smoking weed. Unbothered by them, she continued to swap out her shoes.

"Hey, bitch!" she heard a voice say.

As soon as she turned around... Wham! Someone punched her hard in her face. Nature could hear her teeth shattering. Tasting the bits of splintered teeth in her mouth was one of the absolute worst feelings ever.

She dropped to the ground as excruciating pain shot through her body. Tears raced down her cheeks.

"Help! Somebody, please help me!" Nature hollered at the top of her lungs.

Someone grabbed both of her feet, and her body scraped against the ground, leaving bruises on her stomach and legs as they dragged across the rough and raggedy alley in Baltimore.

"God, please no!" Nature hollered—she was in a tight corner of the alley.

Begging and pleading for her life, she attempted to get up and run but failed. There were way too many of them and only one of her. They yelled and screamed all types of horrible things. She didn't understand why or what she had done to be brutally punished in this way.

Nature's face was pushed even harder into the ground, causing more teeth in her mouth to break.

"No! No-o-o-o!" she hollered out in agony as she felt herself being violated.

The searing pain of a hard, crucial penis invading her rectum was something she had never felt in her life and never wanted to feel again.

"Please! Please!" she cried.

Digging her fingers into the ground due to all the pain, she broke her nails the nail beds.

Nature prayed that everything would be over sooner rather than later. She was confused at that moment about whether she wanted to die or live. Although she loved her life, she didn't know how horribly these animals had destroyed it.

"Nature! Nature!" Her thoughts were interrupted by Michelle.

"I just don't understand, Michelle. Why me? What did I do to deserve this?" Nature cried.

Michelle shook her head back and forth. "I don't give a damn what you did. You didn't deserve this, Nature. No one does, not even a damn animal. But just know that God has a special place in hell for people like this."

"Give me a mirror. I want to see myself," Nature requested.

Michelle sighed deeply as she stared Nature in her mesmerizing brown eyes. Hopelessly, she reached into her oversized bag and pulled out the tiny mirror that she carried around with her.

Sighing again, she remorsefully held it in front of Nature's face.

Nature's hands violently shook as she reached for the mirror. Staring at the tainted and destroyed reflection of herself, she began to shed harsh tears. Her hands began to shake so severely that Michelle had to hold the mirror with a tight grip.

Nature swallowed the lump in her throat. When she opened her mouth and saw all the broken teeth, she felt like she was going to pass out.

The horrible animals who raped and brutally beat her had murdered her conscience, her self-esteem, and practically her entire being.

"I-I..." Nature stuttered. She couldn't speak any words. This was the first time since she had been hospitalized two days ago that she had seen herself in a mirror. She felt like pure shit but didn't have a clue that she looked worse than she felt.

Tears softly started to parade out of Michelle's eyes. She couldn't help but hurt for her friend. Nature's face was messed up pretty badly, and the only thing that would fix it was reconstructive surgery. The doctors had already talked to her family, and that's exactly what they recommended.

"Babe, don't worry. You are pretty as hell. This ain't nothing that surgery can't fix," Michelle assured her.

"Surgery?" Nature repeated.

Michelle nodded. "Yes, surgery. Your parents already agreed. They aren't going to allow their only child to walk around looking all messed up and feeling like shit."

They both laughed. Nature's mother, Veronica, was fly as hell, and you wouldn't catch her ever looking bad. She always made sure she turned heads when she stepped out. She kept herself up so much that everyone always thought she and Nature were sisters rather than mother and daughter. Nature hated that because Veronica clung to that idea and started acting more like Nature's sister than her mother. It was cool and all, but at times, she needed a mother and not a sister or a friend. When those times came around, she was bereft due to Veronica's negligent parenting. Her father, Sam, was no different. He acted as if he didn't know how to love Nature. Not to mention, he was a pushover and a yes man when it came to his wife.

Nature thought about surgery for a while.

"Do you think they will let me..." Nature began but was interrupted when a nurse walked into the room to check her vitals for the thousandth time.

"I'm pretty sure they will. You have them where you want them. Get what you want." Michelle winked.

Nature hated to take advantage of the situation, but since the opportunity had finally presented itself, she was going to do precisely that.

CHAPTER TWO

Across Town - Quest's Apartment...

Tara walked around the room, picking out an outfit and getting herself mentally prepared by smoking some of the best weed that Earth could offer.

Quest lay in bed, exhausted as hell. He thought being an entrepreneur and running his own business would be an easy task, but that wasn't the case at all. His work hours had increased as well as his workload. Free time was so scarce that he barely had time even to sit down and collect his thoughts. But he was confident that hard work would pay off sooner rather than later.

"Tara, I'm thinking about taking a break from work today. Maybe we can do dinner and a movie later?" he said.

Tara glanced at her beeping phone and picked it up, reading the text messages.

"Ummm, babe, I'm not sure. I have so much work to do. Besides, I already made plans with the girls," she stated.

Quest stared at the back of her head. He remembered a few weeks ago when he had mentioned the same thing to Tara, and she came up with a lame excuse.

"Oh, alright. I guess Ron and I will grab a drink or something later."

"Yeah, you and Ron should hang out," Tara agreed.

She put the weed out and set the rest of the blunt in her ashtray. Then she grabbed her towel and went into the bathroom.

As soon as Quest heard the shower running and Tara's vocals blaring through the walls, he jumped up and rushed over to her beeping phone. He hesitated for a moment; he didn't want his sudden insecurities to get the best of him, but something in his gut told him to look through Tara's phone. She was acting weird, and the sudden change had spiked his interest.

Quickly, Quest punched in Tara's unlock code. His heart raced as he scrolled through her cell phone. The first thing he went through was her pictures. He gawked at all the half-naked and naked pictures. And she had plenty of them to view.

"Damn, Tara, why haven't I gotten any of these pictures?" he questioned while stroking his chin hair.

Quest exited the photos and went to the text messages.

He scrolled past all her messages and stopped at the name Nicki. All of Tara's friends were known to him, but Nicki was one that he'd never heard Tara mention.

Growing more furious by the second, Quest read the text messages that this *Nicki* character and Tara had exchanged. All the sexy pictures and *I love yous* pissed him the hell off! He wasn't a damn fool, so he continued to scroll, discovering multiple dick flicks from Nicki. Even worse, he discovered pictures of the guy and Tara together, hugged up and kissing. From the conversations, Quest didn't know if he was the main man or a side piece. Either way, none of the shit sat right with him.

His temperature reached a boiling point as he balled his fists. Quest wanted to drop to his knees and cry, but that crying shit was for weak men, and he was far from weak. The last time he cried was at his parents' double funeral. They died horribly in a car accident. That was eight years ago, and it was the first and last time he'd ever shed a tear. Knowing how hard he loved Tara, how much he provided for her, how much he went out of his way to make her happy, and to see how she took advantage of him pissed Quest the fuck off.

"Tara!" he yelled as he stormed to the bathroom.

He snatched the door open so hard that it hit the wall and left a hole—that was the least of his worries.

"What the fuck is this shit?" he questioned while snatching the shower curtain back.

Startled, Tara jumped as Quest raised the phone to her

face.

"What the hell is this shit, Tara?" he asked again.

Tara turned the water off and sighed deeply. "Quest, why are you going through my phone?" she nonchalantly spoke.

"Fuck why I'm going through your phone! Explain this shit right now!" Quest yelled.

Tara shook her head from side to side.

Quest snatched her towel off the rack and threw it against her chest since she had her hands covering her body as if she didn't want him to look at her. He took a mental note and a quick drive down memory lane. That's when he noticed that for months, Tara had been sleeping with her back turned to him. There was no longer any holding and cuddling. She had been sleeping fully clothed—he couldn't remember the last time he'd felt her naked skin against his flesh.

"Give me my phone, Quest. You should have minded your business."

"Mind my business, Tara? You are in my house, sending another man naked pictures. Telling him you love him and shit."

"Quest, it's over. You should have known that the two of us were over. You really felt like it was okay to neglect me? You don't touch me, kiss me, fuck me, hold me, or anything else, Quest! I been complaining for months, and my complaints fell on deaf ears. You should have known this was going to happen."

Quest stared at Tara like she had three heads. "What the fuck you talking about, Tara? How dare you try to play the damn victim and blame this shit on me! You can't try to justify why you are a fucking whore!"

"A whore? Really? A whore, Quest? Look, I don't have to listen to this shit. Give me two weeks, and I'll be out of your house and your life forever!"

"Two weeks, bitch? You ain't going to be living up in my shit and fucking on another man! You are getting your shit and getting out of my house tonight!" Quest raged.

He slammed Tara's phone down on the sink and rushed out of the bathroom like the mad man he currently was. Back in their bedroom, Quest started grabbing Tara's bags and packing her stuff for her.

Tara stared at her reflection in the mirror; she was happy that Quest had found out about her affair. She didn't know how to break it to him, but she had been unhappy for months. Had he paid her any attention, he would have known that.

"Don't touch my shit!" Tara shouted when she saw Quest running around, grabbing her stuff and throwing it in her little 'spend the night' bags that she had plenty of.

Gripping the towel tightly around her, Tara rushed into the hallway and tried to snatch her bags from Quest.

"You know what, dummy?" Tara mocked through gritted teeth. "Had you been doing your damn job, another man nor the man before him wouldn't have had to do it!"

"Oh, really? You trifling bitch! Let them men take care of

you! You are getting out of my shit today!" Quest harshly grabbed Tara by her arm and started dragging her toward the front door.

Tara began to claw at him, hitting him all over the back of his head. "Get the fuck off me!" she yelled.

Quest turned around, and out of reflex, wham! He knocked Tara across her face, causing her little ass to fall to the floor. Quest had blanked out for a second. He snatched her off the ground like a rag doll and rushed her to the front door. Right in the middle of the winter, twenty-four degrees outside, he threw her out on the cold streets with nothing but her towel wrapped around her.

Tara rushed to the front door and was hit in the face with one of her bags that Quest threw out. Her stuff went flying all over the place, but he didn't give two fucks. He continued to throw her things out the door while she scuffled all over the ground, trying to retrieve her belongings.

"Fuck you, Quest! You won't have no luck!" Tara yelled her final words at him.

"No, fuck you, bitch! You lucky I didn't beat your trifling ass into a coma!" Quest yelled back at her and slammed his front door so hard that a picture of him and Tara fell off the wall and landed on the floor.

He shook his head as he snatched the picture off the floor, then rushed back over to the front door, snatched it open, and threw the photo outside.

CHAPTER THREE

Across Town… Veronica and Sam's Condo

Sam sat back and watched Veronica while she stood in front of him, wearing a pink thong with the matching bra. He loved his wife dearly and would have done anything possible just to make sure she was happy. Too bad the feeling wasn't mutual at all. There were times when he felt like nothing but a meal ticket or maybe even a sugar daddy to Veronica. She barely showed him any love or affection. In fact, she barely touched him or even looked at him.

Sam glanced down at his midsection. He was brick hard at the thought of touching all over Veronica, spreading her legs into an air V, and licking the hell out of her. Making her scream his name as he pleased her. When they first met, she was like a sex-machine. He literally had to take all types of Viagra and shit just to keep up with her ass. Now he was constantly jerking himself off, so much so that his palms had calluses on them from all the hand action he was giving himself.

"Come here for a second. I need your help, Vee," Sam softly moaned.

Veronica walked over to him. With each step she took, her plump ass jiggled and wobbled from side to side.

"What do you need help with?" Veronica asked once she was standing in front of him. She shifted her weight from one leg to the other.

Sam looked down.

Veronica's eyes followed his and landed on his hard manhood. She was hornier than a dog in heat, but she refused to take care of her husband's needs. She loved him and hated him at the same time. The situation was very complicated, but she didn't realize how complicated it was.

"Sam, you know I have to hurry up and get to the hospital to see our daughter. Before I can even go there, I have to stop by the office really quick and take care of some business," she lied.

Sam shook his head. "Come on, Vee. It will only be five minutes," he begged like he usually did.

Veronica sighed, not giving his pleas any thoughts at all. "I really have to go. I'll see you later," she told him and then rushed to get dressed. She settled on a Victoria's Secret sweatsuit and rushed out of the house.

Sam was distraught, but he didn't have it in him to explain to his wife how he felt. So, he did what he usually did. He grabbed his lotion and turned on Pornhub.

"Ugh-h-h-h." He grunted while stroking his manhood up and down. The feeling was so good, but nothing compared to being inside a tight and moist love canal.

He ignored the constant knocks at his door until they could no longer be disregarded.

"Fuck! Every damn time I try to take care of my business, this shit happens!" he fussed as he grabbed his boxers and some sweats. He put them on as he walked to the front door and snatched it open.

"Sorry to bother you, but I have to get some stuff for Nature and take it over to the hospital," Michelle stated while inviting herself in.

Sam didn't say anything as he closed the door back and locked it. He glanced at Michelle's rear end as she walked into Nature's room.

"Damn." He grunted. His mind wandered to places it shouldn't have, but he was like any other man.

"What all do you need?" he questioned while following her.

Michelle stopped in her tracks, and Sam bumped right into her. She turned around, and the two of them stood face to face. They were so close that they could literally taste each other's breath.

"Umm..." Michelle began to stumble over her words.

Sam stood there breathing heavily, looking at Michelle

like she was a snack or perhaps a little more than a snack. He hadn't been that close to a woman in so long, not even his own wife. Veronica left him hanging, and it had been that way for months. She refused to jerk him off, suck his manhood... hell, she refused to even blow on his manhood.

Sam was hungry, so hungry he was ready to feast on just about anything. He aggressively grabbed Michelle by her face and slid his tongue right into her mouth. The two of them exchanged so much saliva as they sucked on each other's tongues.

Sam began to rip at her clothes, and Michelle couldn't climb out of them fast enough.

"Fuck me, big daddy!" Michelle whispered in Sam's ear while biting his earlobe.

Sam was in overdrive as he licked all over Michelle's body. Picking her up, he carried her to his bedroom and laid her on the bed that he and Veronica shared.

Her nipples were so hard and perky that he couldn't resist tasting them. He licked one of her nipples while massaging the other with his hand. His hard manhood brushed against Michelle's thigh. She reached out and grabbed it. It was so hard yet so warm; she wanted it to melt right in her mouth.

Michelle pushed Sam back and dropped to her knees. When she flicked her warm and long tongue across the tip of his hardness, he went so crazy. His eyes rolled, and when she wrapped her tight and wet mouth around it, he couldn't hold back any longer. The sensational feeling drove him utterly insane.

"Ohh-h-h-h! Oh-h-h-h, Michelle," he sensually cried out while making crazy faces.

"Put it inside me," Michelle told him.

Lying on her back, she opened her legs as wide as they could go. Sam climbed on top and slid himself deep inside of her. Michelle was an absolute no no, but for Sam, desperate times called for desperate measures.

He began to stroke her long and hard. She could feel him all in her guts, playing drums with her organs.

"Sam-m-m-m," she softly moaned while flicking her tongue across the top of his ear.

Michelle began to rotate her hips in a circular motion, matching the rhythm that he had created. Together, their bodies moved as if they were one. Sam couldn't hold back any longer; he was already two minutes deep inside of Michelle's love canal, and he felt like he was in heaven.

"Oh, shit! Ugh-h-h-h-h." He grunted while falling on top of Michelle, out of breath.

Michelle wrapped her arms around his waist and rolled her eyes. *I see why his wife cheats on his two-minute ass. The dick is good and big, but his ass don't know how to work the middle at all,* she thought while rolling her eyes.

"Okay, get off me before your wife comes in here and catches us," Michelle said and pushed Sam off her.

She gathered her clothes, then stood in front of Veronica's floor-length mirror and got herself together.

"Sam, this can't happen again," she told him while coating her lips in some thick, cheap lip gloss that she had purchased from the corner hair store.

Sam was so worn out from that little work out that he couldn't possibly pay her any mind.

"I need four hundred dollars, Sam. I need to pay my BGE bill," Michelle mentioned.

Sam looked at her like she was crazy.

"I don't have it, and I think you need to hurry up and get what you came for and go," he told her, quickly switching his entire demeanor.

Sam stared at Michelle and suddenly couldn't stand her. He felt so disgusting and sick that he wanted to vomit. While he harshly stared at Michelle, the two of them didn't know that they had company...

After getting in her car, Veronica felt terrible for the way she treated Sam. She felt that if she wanted to continue receiving gifts, all the pampering and whatnot, she had to at least give him a little pleasure. What would it hurt if she gave him a little hand job here and there? Or at least let him get off by staring at her.

"Sam, Sam, Sam," Veronica softly whispered while shaking her head. She was more than disgusted by Sam's behavior. Fuck him breaking their wedding vows. He was a sick bastard, and as she watched them, Veronica developed even more hatred toward Sam than she already had.

She slowly turned around and tiptoed out of the house, seeing more than she had anticipated.

When she made it to her car, she vomited all over the place. Sam made her beyond sick, and forgiving him was out of the question. Veronica made her mind up at that very moment. Sam was never going to get the opportunity to ever lay a finger on her again. Once she got herself completely together, she would leave him for good.

She got in her car and headed toward her little fling's house. He was always there for her when she needed to clear her mind...

CHAPTER FOUR

Two Years Later...

Quest was a hopeless romantic. He wore his heart on his sleeve, and when he loved, he loved super hard without any questions. Yet, he had his little flaws like everyone else. He catered to his business so much that he forgot to spread his time wisely when it came to a relationship. For that reason alone, he wasn't for the relationship and love shit any longer. Especially after Tara's ungrateful ass broke his heart in so many pieces that he still wasn't able to collect them all. But he was learning how to get over her.

The night Tara left, Quest met a woman, and he found out that fucking someone else's brains out allowed him to get over Tara really quick.

Although he had his moments when he would be down about the situation, the best thing was for him to get underneath another woman to bring him back up. He was hopeless and became dependent on beautiful women and wild nights of fun.

Years later, he was still on his path. Quest had been with so many different women that he had lost count. It wasn't that he didn't want to be with a woman; he just couldn't find that one who held his attention, was genuine, and everything he looked for in a woman. His standards weren't extremely high, but his qualifications were just hard to meet. Until he found someone who could fill that special someone's shoes, he decided to continue dating around.

And dating around is what landed Veronica in his lap.

When Quest first met Veronica, the attraction was fatal. She was built like a stallion and was a big-time freak. The only problem was, Veronica was married, with a whole family.

Quest turned over and faced Veronica, who was scrolling through her cell phone. She was so damn fine, especially to have a child. Her body was perfect, and those childbearing hips of hers drove him insane.

"When are you going to let me hit that all night long until the sun comes up, Vee?" Quest asked while tracing his pointer and middle fingers across her flat stomach.

Veronica looked over at Quest and smiled. She wished she could fulfill Quest's needs, but she wasn't the one.

"Damn, Quest, I would love that. Yet you know that's not

for us. What did we both agree on?" she questioned while leaning next to him and giving him a kiss on his plump lips.

"I know, I know. We can fuck only, but there will never be any strings attached. We are just fuck buddies."

"Right, just fuck buddies. Nothing less and nothing more, Quest."

Veronica got up and started grabbing her clothes. She walked over to the dresser and placed her wedding ring back on her finger. The least she could do was give Sam some sort of respect and not fuck with her wedding ring on. Cheating, she didn't give a fuck about, but she somewhat cared about disrespecting her vows.

Her current mental state was, 'he cheats, and I will cheat back.'

"Look, Veronica, it doesn't matter. With the ring on or off, you are still cheating on your husband," Quest stated while shaking his head and laughing.

Veronica glared at Quest and rolled her eyes.

"You are right, Quest, and we can no longer do this. This guilt is eating me alive.

Quest sighed. "Let me guess, Veronica. You suddenly love your husband now, huh?"

Veronica looked down at her wedding ring. "You know what, Quest? In fact, I do. I love my husband, I love my son, I love my family, and I can no longer do this shit," Veronica forced herself to say.

Quest shook his head from side to side and couldn't hold back the chuckle that escaped from his mouth.

"Oh, after screaming my name at the top of your lungs and me licking you in places the sun don't shine, you suddenly found this profound love for your husband and your family?" Quest was amused. He let out a loud bark of laughter.

"Don't get mad at me, Quest. You are mad cool, fun as hell, and can definitely fuck the brakes off a sister. But I'm not the one for you, babes." She walked over and grabbed his cell phone off the nightstand.

"What are you grabbing my cell phone for?"

Veronica ignored Quest while scrolling through his app store. She typed in POF and started to download it.

"Babe, check this POF shit out. You are looking for love, and I'm not the one. You may find it here on this dating app, but this shit between you and me stops right here and right now," she stated while sliding her shoes on and handing Quest back his cell phone.

Quest looked down at the app.

"Are you out of your mind? Come on now, Vee. Look at me. Do it look like I need a damn dating app?"

Veronica shook her head while grabbing her oversized Louis Vuitton bag and tossing it over her shoulder.

"Don't knock it until you try it, Quest," she told him while pulling her keys out of her bag. She held them in one hand and dug for her oversized sunglasses, which she placed on her face.

"Bye-e-e-e daddy long dick," Veronica teased while blowing Quest a kiss and walking out of his front door.

Quest stared down at the app. "What the hell am I supposed to do with this shit?"

He laughed while allowing his curiosity to get the best of him. In a matter of minutes, he found himself creating a POF profile. Before he knew it, two hours had passed, and he was still scrolling through the app, looking at all the local females who were a match for him, according to POF.

NATURE GLANCED over at Michelle with a smile on her face.

"Michelle, why are you so into your phone? What are you over there smiling about?" She picked up her cup of water and took a sip.

Michelle was cheesing from ear to ear. She was cheesing so hard and so much that her cheeks were starting to ache a bit.

"It's this boy I met on POF. He has my full attention," Michelle answered.

"I bet he does. And what's this POF that you and everyone else keeps talking about?"

"It's a dating app. At first, I thought I would hate it, but I actually ended up liking it. Go ahead and download it, pooh. You'll be surprised what type of fine ass men are on there."

Nature slowly picked her phone up and sat on the thought of going on POF for a few seconds.

"Girl, you better stop playing and download the app.

You know how many good men I ran into on there?" Michelle said.

Nature nodded. "You're right. You have lucked up on there a lot. I'm going to give it a try," she agreed.

She quickly downloaded the app, and before she knew it, she was filling out her profile information. Right after that, she started scrolling through her match pages.

"I don't know about this, Michelle." Nature stared down at her phone, flipping through damn near every picture and pressing the skip button. "Not my type, he looks like a stalker, he looks controlling, ugh I hate dreads, they seem like they are too hard to maintain. Ugh, he looks like a woman abuser." She complained about every man who crossed her screen.

"Damn, Nature, you are being way too picky and judgmental. Give it a chance," Michelle told her.

"I don't see anyone with potential. It's like all of these men are absolutely not my ty..." Her words trailed off as she brought her cell phone closer to her eyes and stared at one man who had finally caught her attention.

"Damn, he is fine," she announced.

Michelle scooted closer to Nature and took the phone out of her hand to get a better view of who she was looking at.

"Mmm hmmm, he's so yummy," Michelle licked her lips and stated, "let's see what he's all about."

The two of them scrolled through his profile, and Michelle read it aloud. Nature loved what she was hearing.

"Looks like you found you a winner after all," Michelle yapped. "Oh my God, Nature. He's messaging you right now!"

Nature gasped and snatched her cell phone out of Michelle's hands to see if she was playing around with her, but that was not the case.

"What the hell? Does this app notify them and let the other party know that their profile is being viewed or something?" Nature questioned.

"I don't think so. That's like violating the privacy act or something, right? But who cares? Read the damn message! And see if he has a friend," Michelle urged.

Nature shook her head. With a broad smile painted on her face, she opened the message.

"Okay, are you ready for this?" Nature questioned and licked her dry lips.

Michelle, all ears, scooted even closer.

"*Hey, beautiful, I know you are probably getting a lot of messages. But I just wanted to tell you the moment I saw your photos, they did a number on my heart. I think it was destined for us to run into each other. By the way, this is my first day on the app, and out of all the females, you are the one who stood out to me the most,*" Nature read aloud.

"Awww, shit, look at him. Trying to be all romantic and shit. Well, go ahead and have your fun, girl. Don't put all of your eggs in one basket." Michelle got up, grabbed her handbag, pulled out her hairbrush, and started brushing through her long, expensive weave.

Meanwhile, Nature was busy texting her new friend back.

Michelle stuck around for a few hours with Nature. She would have stayed the night, but Nature was so invested in her conversation that she figured she would just give her some space.

Nature was relieved when Michelle left. Quest had her full attention, and it was hard for her to focus on anything else. Quest was on point; he didn't even give the conversation a chance to get boring. He replied quickly, and already, he was keeping Nature on her toes—just how she liked things to be.

CHAPTER FIVE

*H*ours later, Quest was still on POF. He found it more interesting than he'd expected. He stopped at a picture of a stunning female and stared at her for a few minutes. She was something that God had taken his time creating. Everything about her seemed so perfect; he instantly started to get a strange tingle in his heart while scrolling through her numerous pictures. Her smile was one of a kind. It could take the most broken person out of a place they thought they couldn't break free from. Her smile was contagious, and it had the effect of lighting up an entire room.

"Nature," Quest read her name aloud. "What a unique and beautiful name for such a stunning woman," he mentioned.

Scrolling through her profile, he started to read everything. *I'm on here just because I was referred to this app by a few people. I would hate to say that I'm on here in search of my Romeo. But hey, if it happens, then I am down. I love to read deep, dark poetry, play in makeup, shop, spend time with my best friend, self-care, and educate myself as much as I can. I strongly believe that conversation runs the nation. Please, no creeps, catfishes, phonies, or men who are just looking for sex. I'm very unique and fragile, so it's a must that you be careful with me. Sorry if this sounds silly. But hey, that's me!*

Quest read her profile over and over as he pondered if he should contact her or not.

"What the hell, why not? What do I really have to lose?" Quest spoke before sending her a message.

Hey, beautiful, I know you are probably getting a lot of messages. But I just wanted to tell you the moment I saw your photos, they did a number on my heart. I think it was destined for us to run into each other. By the way, this is my first day on the app, and out of all the females, you are the one who stood out to me the most, Quest keyed into the message box. He thought for a second and wondered if he sounded a bit cheesy or perhaps pressed. Seizing the moment, he shrugged and pressed the send button.

Quest was really surprised when Nature replied right back to him in a matter of seconds.

Hey, tell me more. What kind of number did they do on you? I'm very interested. What are you doing on here? What are you looking for? What do you like to do for fun?

Quest quickly messaged her back, and four hours later,

they were still messaging about any and every little thing they could think about.

Quest's days were now a lot happier. He ended up cutting off many of the females that he was dealing with. His one-night stands were slowly but surely coming to a complete stop because Nature was taking up so much of his time. Months had passed, and he was still interested in her. He loved the way the two of them carried on. Their online relationship went from sending messages back and forth on POF to voice messages. They then moved to phone texts and then right to phone calls which would last for hours. The two of them felt like they couldn't go about their day without speaking.

The conversation wasn't the only thing that kept them going. They knew how to keep each other entertained.

Quest stepped out of the shower, stood in front of his wide mirror, and stared at his reflection.

"Are you out of the shower now? What are you doing?" Nature asked over the phone.

Quest smiled at himself in the mirror. "I'm standing in the mirror, looking at myself. Did you get out of the shower yet?" he questioned.

Nature smiled. She was out of the shower, lying across her bed, butt naked.

"Yes, babe. I been out," she softly moaned.

"Mmm, I hear that. What do you have on?"

"Nothing." Nature sighed.

"Oh, is that right?" Quest quickly began to envision

Nature's bare flesh. He imagined touching all over her body and softly gliding his tongue over her smooth skin. Pleasing her in every way possible.

The erotic thoughts caused his manhood to get brick hard.

"Damn, baby, you got me over here hot," Quest admitted.

Nature bit her bottom lip and rubbed her hands between her thighs.

"God, daddy, I am so fucking wet. I just keep imagining you fucking me. I want you so bad, babe," Nature squealed.

Quest rushed to his room and lay in his bed. His dick was so hard that there was only one thing he could do about it while he imagined Nature there next to him.

He wrapped his strong hand around his thick and hard manhood. Grabbing his lotion, he squirted just enough to get things going in a good motion. He slowly began moving his hand up and down.

"Oh, shit, Nature. You got my dick so damn hard over here," he told her while stroking his manhood.

"Do I, baby? Show me, please. Let me see how hard my dick is," she softly cooed.

Quest snapped a picture of his hardness and sent it to Nature.

"Oh, babyyy-y-y-y. It's so fucking hard and big. I want to feel it inside of me so bad. I want to wrap my mouth around it and suck all the cum out. Please, baby, I need it," Nature moaned.

Quest began to stroke himself faster and much harder. "Yeah, that's what you want to do. Tell me what else you want to do."

"Oh, baby, my pussy is so wet. I got two of my fingers deep inside of me. It's so damn wet. Please make me cum, baby," Nature moaned.

"That's right, baby. Massage that clitoris and slide your finger deep inside. Just imagine me inside you. Do you feel this big dick inside of you? Does it feel good? I want you to cum all over this dick."

"Oh, God, I feel it, Quest! I feel it all inside of me. Oh-h-h-h-h, I'm about to cum all over your big dick. I'm cuming, Quest!" Nature cried.

Quest wrapped his hands tightly around his manhood and began stroking it up and down a bit faster. He was so into it, beyond horny, and didn't stop until his cum shot out the tip of his penis like a geyser.

"Oh, shit, Nature! I'm cuming," he moaned as the palms of his hands filled with all of his babies.

"Mmm, that felt so good, baby," Nature gasped.

Quest nodded his head, agreeing with her. "Yeah, that felt really good. But I can't wait until I meet up with you and finally see you in person, so we can do all this stuff to each other. It's been months now. When will we see each other?" he asked.

Nature bit her bottom lip. Quest wasn't really pressuring her into meeting, but there were times when he did ask.

"Really soon, baby. I have a very important work trip

that I have to take in a few weeks. After that, I can give you all my attention, and we can meet up," she told him.

"Alright, I hear you," Quest stated. He got out of bed, grabbed a washcloth, and cleaned himself off.

"Okay, baby, you wore me out tonight. I'm going to get some sleep, so I can get up for work in the morning," Nature said.

"Alright, I love you."

"I love you more," she replied and ended the call.

Quest lay across his bed, staring up at the ceiling. At times he felt crazy for falling deeply in love with a woman that he had never seen in person and whom he had never physically touched. But the feelings were just way out of his control. His heart wanted what his heart wanted, and that was Nature.

CHAPTER SIX

$\mathcal{N}$ature got out of her bed, snatched her favorite white and black teddy bear, and held it tightly in her arms as she stared out of the window. Tears slowly paraded from the corners of her eyes as she listened to her parents argue. It was something they did all the damn time, and it was driving her insane. They seemed to argue about everything little thing, and this particular morning, she needed them to be in good spirits.

They were too selfish to understand how badly Nature really needed them; this was the morning that she had prayed for yet feared. This was the morning of her surgery. Once she got her surgery, she would finally be able to look in the mirror and love the reflection that stared back at her. Not look in the mirror and feel pure hatred.

"Come on now, Veronica. She doesn't need all that extra surgery. She needs to love who she is," Sam argued.

Veronica loved her child and would do anything in the world to make Nature happy, especially if the expenses weren't on her.

"Really, Sam? How dare you say that shit! Look at her, always walking around, looking all sad and shit. Them animals messed her life up completely. As her parents, we are the ones who must fix her life. And if you don't pay for the surgery, then I'm going to do whatever it takes to make sure our daughter is happy," Veronica argued.

Sam grabbed his tie and wrapped it around his neck.

Veronica walked over to him. Truthfully, she wanted to take that tie and strangle him to death. But, as his wife, she did her part and tied his tie like she did every morning before he went to work. Or at least on the mornings when she didn't leave before him.

Sam sighed deeply as he slid on his slacks. When it came to arguing and stuff like that, he always resisted a bit. Yet, in the end, Veronica always received the victory.

"What do you want me to do, Vee?" He stood and zipped his pants.

Veronica wore a smile across her face; as always, it was her way. "I want you to do whatever makes our daughter happy."

"You mean—" Sam began.

Veronica walked over and placed her lips against his, causing him to be quiet. She slid her tongue deep into his mouth, and their tongues danced together for a few seconds.

"Thank you, Sam. I love you." She kissed his lips while holding the sides of his face.

"I love you too," Sam replied.

Veronica walked into Nature's room, catching her standing at her window, holding her teddy bear.

Nature wiped her tears and turned around to face her mom.

"Awww, baby, today is one of the best days of your life. Wipe your tears and be happy," Veronica told her daughter.

She walked over to Nature and wiped the remainder of her tears from her eyes.

"I know. I just hate when you and Daddy argue all the time. I hate when you two argue about me," Nature admitted.

"Oh, Nature, baby, this doesn't have anything to do with you. Your dad and I are at that point where we bump heads a lot. That's just the way things sometimes go when you are with a person for so long," Veronica said.

Veronica stopped in front of the mirror and smiled at the beautiful reflection that stared back at her. Admiring herself for a moment, she forgot all about Nature. She was somewhat obsessed with herself because she hadn't always been beautiful. It took a lot of lying on someone's table and a lot of money to achieve the beauty that she possessed. She had a nice body, curves to die for, and an ass that stuck out so far that you could literally put a cup on it. Veronica had the perfect sized breasts that Sam had paid nearly ten thousand dollars for, and he couldn't even touch them if his life depended on it.

So, when Nature talked so much about surgery, she understood completely. Veronica felt that everyone should do whatever would make them happy. They were the rightful owner of their body and any modifications to it.

"Well, babe, I didn't come in here for this. I wanted to talk to you before your surgery. I wanted to let you know that surgery changes you dramatically. Some people forget who they are after they have such a drastic change. Sweetie, I want to tell you that I love you, and I just want you to be transparent at all times and love yourself. I don't want you to lead yourself or anyone on without being honest."

Nature stared her mother up and down. She had to admit that ever since her mother got her body done, she had become a totally different person. The way she talked, the way she dressed, and the places she went. She just wasn't the same any longer, and Nature vowed to herself that she wouldn't fall in those shoes. Nature wouldn't stray from the truth.

"Do you understand, sweetie? Can we make that agreement?"

Nature walked over to her mother and wrapped her arms around her. "I understand, Mom, and yes, it's an agreement."

"Good. You should go in there and have a talk with your father, and then we can get going," Veronica suggested.

While Nature was in the other room, talking with Sam, Veronica went to the bathroom, dropped to her knees, and said a quick prayer for Nature. Asking God to protect her and let her have a good surgery with a speedy recovery.

NATURE STOOD in her private room and stripped down to her birthday suit. She stared at her reflection in the mirror, saying goodbye to the person in front of her. She couldn't wait to welcome and embrace the new and 'improved' Nature that was steps away from happening.

She grabbed her cellphone and sent Quest a text message.

Hey, babe, I'm getting on my flight now. My boss has this policy of no phones, so I will talk to you in two-three weeks. Love you.

She turned her cell phone off and sighed. It hurt like hell, lying to Quest and not being completely transparent about so many things, yet it hurt even more that she would have to go two to three weeks without talking to him.

"If he loves me, he will wait for me," Nature told herself.

Minutes later, Nature was lying on the surgery table with so many people surrounding her. She was scared as hell. Her heart was racing so fast that she thought it indeed would race right out of her chest. Yet, Nature was doing exactly what she wanted and what she felt she needed to do.

"Hey, there, how are you? Can you please state your full name and your birthdate?" a nurse sat next to Nature and asked...

CHAPTER SEVEN

Nature slowly opened her eyes and had no clue where she was. Hell, she didn't know if she was dead or alive until an enormous amount of excruciating pain shot through her entire body. She felt like she had been hit by a car or something. When she tried to sit up, she could barely move. The room was pitch black, and the only sound was the machines beeping. She opened her mouth to say something and noticed that her throat was super dry.

"Nurse! Mommy! Somebody!" Nature hollered, and she didn't recognize her own voice. It came out in a raspy whisper.

Seconds later, a nurse popped up. "Hey, there! Glad you're up. How are you feeling?" she questioned.

Nature stared at her. "I feel like I'm near death," she gasped.

"Okay, so your pain is on what level from one to ten?" She grabbed her notepad and pen.

"A fucking ten. I need something bad. Please!" Nature cried.

"Okay, no problem. I will get you something now and get your doctor," she told Nature and disappeared.

After Nature took her pain meds, she felt much better. She couldn't wait to get out of the recovery room and get to her actual room, so she could rest and get a bit more comfortable.

The next day, Nature felt miserable as hell and full of regrets. She kept telling herself that the pain wouldn't last forever and it would all be over soon. Those words of encouragement that she told herself didn't do much for her, though. The next day, she declined all visitors, although the only two people who came to visit were Michelle and her mother. Still, all she wanted to do was lie in bed, soak in her own misery, and cry her pain away.

On day four, she felt a little better. She was able to sit up in bed and sip some soup.

"Hey, sunshine! How are you feeling today?" Michelle walked into the hospital room with a bouquet of flowers. She set the flowers on the table next to Nature, then went over to the window and opened the curtains. The instant sunlight caused Nature's eyes to ache. Truthfully, she had kept the curtains closed and hadn't seen any sun in days.

"I'm doing okay, Michelle, but I'm still in a lot of pain. My doctor keeps telling me that it will get so much better in a few days, and I can't wait for those days to arrive!" Natured cried.

"Yeah, it will be better really soon, babe. Just remember, we are the strongest of them all, and beauty is pain," Michelle told her.

Nature stared off into space for a few moments, thinking about Michelle's words.

"Hey, why don't we get you out of this bed and walk around the hospital for a bit?" Michelle suggested.

Nature shrugged. "I just want to lay here."

"Yeah, you may just want to lay there, but you won't. Remember, the more you lay around, the more your body will hurt."

Michelle walked over to Nature, snatched the covers off her, and began to help her out of bed.

"Wait. Girl, what happened to your face?" Nature questioned, catching a quick glimpse of Michelle's face.

She noticed that Michelle's eye was black, and no matter how much makeup she tried to wear, she couldn't hide that black eye from her best friend.

Michelle sighed deeply. "Love, you have to be careful. Some love you but don't know how to love you. And then you got some who are afraid to love you. This is the reaction of one that's afraid," Michelle confessed.

Nature shook her head. "Stop telling yourself that bullshit, Michelle. Love isn't supposed to hurt!" she insisted.

"Look, girl, stop it. I'm here for you and your health. We will talk about me later." Michelle brushed it off and helped

Nature slide on her bedroom slippers. "So, have you talked to your lover boy Quest yet?" she questioned.

At the mention of Quest's name, Nature's heart began to beat extra fast. A smile crept across her face. "No, but I did turn my phone on today. He'd texted me every day, telling me how much he loves me and misses me. I think he's the one," Nature spoke. She held her hand close to her heart as she stole a few seconds to fantasize about Quest.

"He seems like a pretty good guy, and I'm happy for you."

"Yeah, thank you. Now, let's go back to the room. Everything hurts," Nature began to complain.

Michelle stopped in front of her and bent down. "You want a ride back?" She patted her hips and giggled.

Nature laughed. "Bitch, you know I'm too big to get on your back." Yet she hopped on and nearly hurt herself, trying to get onto Michelle's back.

"Oh my God, what are you trying to do? Knock me over?" Michelle laughed. "Oh, my God! Girl, you are going to break my back," she joked.

"Stop playing, Michelle. I'm not that heavy. Now you going to make me go on a diet or go on a food strike or something."

Michelle gave her a piggyback ride all the way back to her room.

"When I ask you for a piggyback ride, you better return the favor too, Nature. And I'm not playing with you," Michelle mentioned.

"Trust me, I got you, boo."

When they got back to the room, Nature handed Michelle her cell phone and let her read all the text messages that she and Quest had sent to each other over the past few months.

Michelle got lost in reading the messages. The love between the two of them was evident in their words. She was a hopeless romantic, and what Nature had was exactly what she wanted. Michelle was happy for her best friend. She gazed up from the cell phone to check on Nature, and she was knocked out sleeping.

Michelle curled up in the chair next to her friend and finished reading the text messages until she too fell asleep.

CHAPTER EIGHT

*Q*uest looked down at his cell phone and couldn't believe the message that he read. After all this time, finally, the love of his life was ready to meet up with him. Nature telling him that she was ready to meet up made him the happiest man in the world.

When can we meet up? Quest texted.

Tonight. Let's meet downtown at the Harbor. How about around 7:30PM? Nature texted back.

Quest had plans with Ron and the boys, but he was willing to cancel everything for Nature.

That's a date. See you tonight. Quest texted back.

He rushed to the shower, and after showering and getting dressed, he was off to the barbershop. To him, first impressions were always the best, and he wanted to be as handsome as he could be when he met Nature for the very first time.

Before he knew it, the time had approached. Heading toward the Harbor, he stopped and purchased Nature a bouquet of flowers. As he drove to the destination, his heart was in the pit of his stomach. He was consumed by a mixture of emotions, and the thing that sat on his mind the most was the possibility that Nature was a catfish. All he kept thinking about was if she wasn't who she said she was. He wondered if she was someone else hiding behind the pictures.

"Man, let me stop this shit. I'm in love with the woman who I got to know. Looks don't matter," Quest told himself as he pulled into an empty parking spot.

He truly meant those words. Quest was in love with Nature, and if she pulled up looking like some Sumo wrestler with no edges, he was still going to love her for who she was.

His phone rang, and he immediately answered.

"Hey, babe, I'm here. Where are you?" Nature questioned.

Quest was smiling from ear to ear. "I'm in the end parking lot, in a white Mercedes Benz. I'm ready to get out now," he told her.

"Okay, I see you. Here I come," she replied.

Quest checked himself out in the mirror, making sure he didn't have anything on his face. He looked at his hat and noticed it had some white spots on it. "Shit!" he cursed as he mentally beat himself up for scarfing down the two powdered donuts while getting dressed. "Great, now this looks like some damn cum or something." He embarrassedly shook his head.

He tried to wipe the spots off, but they wouldn't budge. Once he took his hat off, Quest noticed that he had accidentally cut his head while shaving it bald. He quickly pondered whether he should wear the hat. He would much rather Nature see the spot on his hat versus seeing the big gash on his bald head that he was sporting. So, he kept the hat on and jumped out of the car. After a quick breath check, he snatched the flowers off the seat and stood in front of the vehicle.

Nature sat in her car and looked herself over. She was so gorgeous that it didn't make any sense. Her smile was breathtaking, and her energy matched it.

She grabbed her cell phone and called Michelle. "Hey, boo. I'm here to meet him now," Nature said.

Michelle giggled. "Girl, you are really tripping. I'm parked right beside you. I got your back, and I got my pepper spray just in case he's a lunatic or something," she told her as she tightly gripped her pepper spray.

"Right, I am being so silly. Wish me luck," Nature said.

"Good luck. Go ahead and get your man."

It's now, or never, Nature told herself as she stepped out of the car and started walking toward Quest's car.

The moment the two of them saw each other, both of their hearts dropped. The moment felt so surreal. Quest stared at Nature; she was so beautiful. The pictures didn't do her any justice whatsoever.

"Quest?" Nature squealed.

"Nature?"

They rushed over to each other, and Quest snatched Nature off the ground. Wrapping his arms tightly around her, he spun Nature in a circle.

"Oh my God. Quest, after a year and a half, I finally get to see you in person. I finally get to hold you and touch you," Nature cooed as tears fell from her eyes. She was such an emotional creature.

"Damn, Nature, it's really been that long. Miss Want to Hide Behind the Phone and not see your man," Quest told her.

He hated that he hadn't met Nature sooner. Truth be told, if his heart wasn't so invested, he would have already kicked her to the curb for hiding behind the phone. Quest was a very handsome man with good vibes. He had no need for internet or phone dating, but he'd fallen in love knee-deep with Nature, so he decided to play those little waiting games with her. From the looks of things, she was worth the wait.

Quest stared Nature up and down and licked his lips. Temptation was a mother fucker. There were so many nasty things that he wanted to do to her and with her at that moment. He had to pump his brakes a bit in order to contain himself.

"Damn, babe, those pictures didn't do you any justice at all! You look so good. Thick in all the right places," Quest complimented.

Nature was all smiles, and she instantly began to blush. "Thank you, babe. I had to make sure you wasn't a stalker or a catfish or a weirdo," she said.

"Oh, these are for you." Quest ignored her comment and handed her the flowers.

Nature held them to her nose and inhaled their fresh scent. "Thank you. These are so beautiful." Little gestures like that melted her heart and won her completely over.

Nature had never received flowers from anyone. Little did she know, the way she had Quest's heart, there would be so much more pampering and gifting to come in due time.

"Come on, let's go for a walk," Quest suggested.

"A walk? Babe, it's cold outside," Nature replied with a wide smile.

Quest looked her up and down again, undressing her with his eyes. "I mean, we can either go for a walk and have a talk. Or I can umm... take you back home and do a bunch of pleasant things to you."

"Stop it, Quest," Nature cooed. "I'm going to take you up on that walk."

As they walked across the street, hand in hand, Nature glanced back to where Michelle was parked and threw her thumb up behind her back.

Michelle beeped her horn by accident. She had been sitting in the car, watching everything, and she was so excited for her best friend. At the same time, she was kind of sad. Michelle so badly wanted the love that Nature had. Her heart craved it; she went to bed at night, thinking about being in the arms of a strong man who loved her and took care of her heart. She woke up, still with that mystery man occupying space in her mind.

Quest held Nature's hand tightly as they walked toward the inner harbor. It was so beautiful out. The spot they were standing in overlooked the water and provided a view of Baltimore's beautiful skyline.

"This is so beautiful," Nature stated.

"Yeah. I guess Baltimore has something beautiful besides you to offer," he flirted.

Quest stopped in his tracks and turned around to face Nature. The moon was so bright; it bounced off Nature's glossy lips, causing her to light up a bit.

"I love you, Nature," Quest whispered and leaned forward.

It was like magic as their lips magnetically connected. Quest slid his tongue in Nature's mouth, allowing their tongues to dance to their special love tune. With the exchange of love energy, they both could feel the magnetic transfer running through their veins. Nature's skin hairs happily stood, and Quest, on the other hand, was rock hard. He could literally break something with the hardness of his penis.

They stood there for every bit of ten minutes, trading energy and rubbing each other. Both of them had forgotten that they were standing outside in the middle of winter at the inner harbor. Yet, they didn't care. Nope, they didn't care not one bit about how cold it was, nor did they care that people had stopped and were watching them, enjoying the PG-13 show that the two of them were putting on.

"Oh my God, Quest. I want you forever," Nature admitted.

Quest grabbed her by her chin and stared deep into her eyes, penetrating her soul. "If you want me forever, then you have me forever," he sternly spoke.

Whew! That meant so much to Nature. Her heart began to thump at a fast pace as if a marching band was in it.

"Quest, wow. I don't know what to say," Nature replied.

Quest leaned in again and exchanged a few wet kisses with Nature on her lips.

"Please, Nature, tell me that you will let me take you home with me. I want you in my arms right now, and I don't want to ever let you go," Quest admitted.

Nature was in a place that she had never been in before. Mentally, she was finally happy. Quest had her heart, and she had his. The two of them shared a love that neither of them had ever experienced in the past. They both were scared as hell but were ready to risk everything just to have a shot at love.

"Okay, babe, give me your address, and I'll meet you there in thirty minutes," Nature told Quest.

Quest nodded. "Good, that gives me time to clean up my little bachelor pad," he joked.

He grabbed her hand and led her back across the street to her car.

"Thirty minutes, Nature. You better not be late, or I'm

going to come and find you," Quest joked, but he really meant it.

Nature started her car. "Okay, I will see you in thirty minutes, babe," she told him. As she began to pull off, Quest rushed over to her car and snuck another kiss.

"See you in thirty minutes," he repeated.

Quest got in his car and pulled off. Once he was gone, Michelle pulled up with tears in her eyes...

NATURE WALKED AROUND HER ROOM, packing her overnight bag. "Michelle, God is good. Dreams do come true. Did you see how handsome Quest is? I can't believe he's like real," Nature gushed while walking from one side of the room to the other.

Nature had been babbling off about Quest so much. Michelle was happy for her, but at the same time, she just couldn't bear too much of Nature talking about Quest.

"Girl, you better shut up and pack your little spend the night back quickly. You know your man is waiting for you." Michelle tried her best to brush the conversation off and change the topic.

"Quest is just everything... everything, Michelle. I'm so much in love." Nature held a shirt in her hand and stared off into love land.

"Wait, where is your mom, Nature?" Michelle questioned, yet again hoping to brush off the conversation.

"What's today? Oh yeah, she's on a business trip for the next three days," Nature answered.

Michelle nodded and gazed down at her cell phone.

"You know what? Fuck it, Michelle. I'm going all the way out for my man tonight. I'm wearing this, my long coat, and some heels. He's about to be in for a surprise." Nature smirked while holding up a sexy little red lace lingerie set.

"Now that's what I am talking about!" Michelle said while reading the text message that was sent to her. "Go all the way out for him!"

Michelle put her phone down and walked over to Nature's bag. She started throwing stuff in there that Nature might need.

"Never keep a man waiting for too long," she told her.

Nature smiled while changing into the outfit of her choice.

"How do I look?" Nature questioned.

Michelle clapped her hands. "Turn around."

Nature spun around, showcasing her thick thighs and all her curves.

"Yess, bitch! Yess! You look so good I want to fuck you myself!" Michelle playfully stated while smacking Nature on her plump ass.

"Okay, good. Let me hurry up and go. I don't want to keep my man waiting for too long." Nature scooped up her overnight bag, then grabbed her cell phone and charger.

Little did she know, she had already kept Quest waiting eight minutes too long. He was anxiously pacing his wooden floors, debating whether to call Nature or give her a few more minutes. Part of him believed that she wouldn't dare stand him up because of the connection they shared, but the other part kept telling him that he had been stood up.

"Wait, are you going to tell him?" Michelle asked, stopping Nature in her tracks.

"That I'm a virgin? He's going to find out very soon if you let me go!" She giggled. Nature rushed over to Michelle, hugged her tightly, and kissed her on her cheeks. "I love you, and I will text you when I get over there."

Nature was in such a rush that she forgot Michelle didn't live there. She didn't offer to walk down with her to the lobby like they always did or anything like that. Everything was about Quest, which Michelle understood. Her best friend was in love and living her best life at that moment.

Nature rushed out of the front door. Once she got to the elevator of her parents' luxurious condo that overlooked Baltimore City, she became antsy. The elevator took its time climbing up to the fifty-eighth floor.

"Fuck this!" Nature told herself and rushed to the stairs. Then she realized that she would get all sweaty. She didn't want to show up at her man's house, smelling like a grown ass man who had been working hard all day and night.

She rushed back to the elevators and caught them just in time.

MICHELLE WALKED BACK to Nature's room, passing Sam and Veronica's bedroom.

Once she got into Nature's room, she walked over to her bed and began to put all of Nature's clothes away that she had thrown all over the bed and floor. She picked up a sexy one-piece of lingerie. Smiling, she decided, why not?

Michelle slowly climbed out of her clothes and slid it on. She stared at her reflection in the floor-length mirror and was happy with her overall appearance. Although she did find some flaws that she wanted to work on, Michelle wasn't going to tear herself down and worry about the things that she couldn't change at that time. Instead, she decided to love herself more and embrace all her imperfections.

"Damn, you look so fine," a voice said.

Michelle immediately turned around and noticed Sam watching.

She stared at him; her eyes scanned his entire body. He had nothing on but his birthday suit, and she loved every inch of it. His manhood was standing at attention, saluting her. Begging her to come and give it some attention.

"Really, Sam? Are you just saying that, or do you really mean it?" Michelle questioned.

Sam reached out and motioned for her to come to him. "I mean it, Michelle. You know I do."

Michelle turned around and stared back into the mirror. She couldn't control it. Maybe that's why she and Nature were so close. They both were emotional as heck. Tears slowly danced out of her eyes.

"Then why you did me the way you did me last time? A man who loves a woman would never beat on her," Michelle told him.

Sam walked over and stood behind her.

Michelle's breathing picked up.

He was so close to her; she could feel his penis poking her in the back. She could feel his breath on the back of her neck.

Sam wrapped his arms around her waist. "Take my word, Michelle. I'm so sorry, and it will never happen again. I was angry, confused, and just wasn't myself at that moment. You have to understand me!" he exclaimed.

"If you are questioning it or doubting it, then why are you here with me right now?" Michelle questioned.

As always, Sam ignored the questions and lured her in with his warm tongue, his touches, and kisses.

He began to kiss Michelle on the back of her neck as his hands roamed over her body.

"Make me feel good," he told Michelle as he helped her turn around.

At that moment, Michelle forgot all about how poorly Sam had treated her. She forgot all about Sam being a married man, and most of all, she forgot about Sam being her best friend's father. The only thing that mattered was that a man loved her.

She dropped to her knees and slowly took Sam's warm,

thick manhood into her mouth. Inch by inch until it all disappeared. Her head bobbed up and down as she nearly swallowed his manhood whole like a boa constrictor, and her warm, wet mouth wrapped tightly around it like a python.

"Oh, Michelle. Ohh shit-t-t-t," Sam cried. He couldn't hold it back a second longer.

Although Michelle had started engaging in the throat action no longer than two minutes ago, his warm protein filled her mouth and throat. Michelle swallowed it in one gulp, showing Sam how nasty she was willing to be for him.

Michelle walked over to the bed and slid out of the little outfit she had on. She got on the edge of the bed and bent over on all fours, then smacked her rear end.

"Put it right here, daddy," Michelle seductively whispered.

Sam rushed over and did exactly what she told him to do.

"Sam! Sam, I love you so much!" Michelle cried as he filled her insides with his joystick.

Each pump, each stroke, she fell deeper and deeper in love with someone else's husband.

The strokes felt so damn good that she didn't have a second to even consume any guilt. Her only thoughts were about cuming all over his stick.

Sam leaned forward and sucked all over her back. Reaching under her, he grabbed her nipples and began to squeeze them tightly between his thumb and pointer fingers.

"Tell me you love me!" he demanded.

"I love you," she replied.

Sam grabbed her plump ass and slapped it harshly a few times. Tightly grabbing her waist, he began to stroke even harder and faster.

"Ohh-h-h, Sam!" Michelle cried as she squirted her love juices all over him.

She grabbed her butt cheeks and spread them, giving Sam more access than needed to her warm haven. Sam was more than happy to hear those words; he was holding on to all that he had left in him.

He let go. "Ughh-h-h-h," he roared as he released into Michelle.

They both collapsed on the bed, and that's when guilt consumed them.

Michelle got up and quickly began to grab her stuff. "Let me go. I have work early in the morning," she lied.

Truth be told, she was an emotional wreck, and like always, she felt heartbroken when the fun was over, and reality sunk it. She left with no man, no plans, no nothing, as always.

Michelle was more than tired of selling herself short. She was beyond exhausted from playing the side chick, sneaking and creeping, all to still be in love with someone else's man, who would never truly love her properly or be with her. Michelle was far from a fool; the writing was on the wall. Sam was never going to leave his wife, and as long as she continued to play the side chick, he would continue to play with her and discard her when it was time to cater to his wife. In her eyes, side chicks never won. Even when they thought they were winning, they actually were losing...

CHAPTER NINE

*N*ature pulled up to Quest's house, feeling like a little kid on Christmas who just knew she was going to receive everything on her Christmas list, whether she was naughty or nice. She pulled out her cell phone to text Quest. Looking down at her phone, she quickly keyed in the message. Just as she was about to hit the send button, she was startled by a knock on her window, nearly scaring the soul out of her body.

"Oh shit, babe, you scared me." Nature jumped. She was more than thankful that it was Quest and not some stranger trying to rob her or something.

"Come on, it's cold out here," Quest told her and opened her car door.

Nature grabbed her bag and handed it to him.

When she got out of the car, she trailed closely behind

Quest to the steps of his house. She glanced down at his feet and noticed that he didn't have any shoes on.

"You came out here in your bare feet?" she asked.

Quest shook his head. "In my mother fucking bare feet."

"Love will make you do some crazy things, huh?" Nature quipped.

"Do you want a drink or anything? You can take your bag upstairs, and I'll be right there."

"I'll have whatever you're having, and where's your bathroom?" Nature asked.

"Upstairs. Make your first right, and you'll see my bedroom and the bathroom right there."

Nature turned around and began to saunter up the stairs. She admired Quest's home and was really impressed with how clean he kept the house. She was a super neat freak and had a crazy low-key OCD. When she rubbed her hand across the step's railing, she looked down and didn't see a hint of dust or dirt. Nature was more than pleased.

She walked to his bedroom, happy that it was spotless. After neatly placing her bag on a nearby chair, she walked into the bathroom.

Hmm, a clean bathroom too. That's twenty points for you, Mr. Quest, she thought. Nature didn't really have to use the bathroom. She decided to hide in there for a few minutes. She waited patiently until she heard Quest's footsteps walking around the room, so she could step out and surprise him.

"Hey, Nature girl, what are you doing in there? You

better not be funking up my bathroom and stopping my toilet up," Quest joked.

Nature smiled and bit her bottom lip. "Here I come, babe," she answered. She flushed the toilet and ran the water like she was washing her hands.

Slowly, she strutted out of the bathroom, both excited and nervous at the same time.

As she stood in the doorway, Quest was busy reading a novel that he found deeply interesting. Seeing her shadow against the wall, he looked up in her direction.

"Oh, shit!" Quest said and slid the book to the side.

Nature stood there, looking so damn edible.

She dropped her coat, and it gently landed on the wooden floor. "Is this what you've been waiting for?" she whispered while seductively biting her bottom lip.

Nature turned around so he could get a look at everything she had to offer. Poking her ass out, she bent over and touched her toes.

She was driving Quest insane. He jumped up, ready to pounce on Nature.

"Calm down, bad boy," Nature teased.

She stepped over her coat and strutted over to him.

Quest couldn't fight the temptation. He wanted Nature badly. Even more, he needed her. He grabbed the sides of her face and slid his tongue deep into her mouth.

Soft, passionate moans escaped both their mouths.

"How do you get out of this?" Quest blurted out as he fumbled with Nature's outfit. He had no clue how she put it on, let alone how he was going to take it off. "Fuck it!" he murmured as he tore the lace.

Quest laid her on the bed and removed his clothing. Nature stared at his huge, God-given blessing with lust and excitement. Climbing on top of Nature, he slowly planted soft kisses all over her face, her neck, and then worked his way down her entire body. He wanted to touch every inch of her, not leaving any parts of her body untouched. Quest got down to her paradise and kissed her inner thighs.

Nature's heart pounded; she was in a place she never thought she would be in.

Quest ran his warm tongue down Nature's thighs. When he got to her feet, surprisingly, he shoved one of her toes into his mouth and began to suck it.

"Oh, shit!" Nature cooed. "Oh, so you nasty nasty." She laughed.

"You ain't seen nothing yet. I'm trying to give you all my love," Quest confessed.

And that he did. He went back to her paradise and spread her thighs as wide as they could go. He dove into her pool filled with nothing but the purest love juices and traced his tongue around her protruding clitoris. Softly, he sucked on it. Her clitoris was throbbing like it had its own heartbeat. Quest began to beat softly on it with his tongue, attempting to make it explode.

Moving down to her sweet opening, he softly slid his tongue deep inside.

"Oh, I love you!" Nature squealed. Grabbing her nipples, she squeezed them tightly.

"I... love... you... too... Nature," Quest replied between licks and slurps.

Nature grabbed the sheets; she felt like she was going to explode all over the place.

Quest went back to her throbbing clitoris, flicking his tongue around it in a circular motion. He then slid two of his fingers inside Nature.

His fingers made her tense up a little, and Quest felt it too.

Nature never had fingers inside of her before. Of course, she had explored her own body with fingering around the clitoris and maybe a little at the opening of her love canal. But this was the first time anything had been inside of it.

"Damn, you are so tight and wet. You feel like a virgin," Quest said.

Nature bit her bottom lip, debating whether she should tell him. At that moment, she made the conscious decision to be completely transparent with her lover.

"I am a virgin," she admitted.

Quest was surprised, yet the proof was right between her thighs. That very second, he knew she was the one. She was the one he wanted forever. Nature was pure, untainted, and she was his. He sucked hard on her clitoris and slid his finger deep inside of her, touching her G-spot.

"Oh, Quest-t-t-t! Quest-t-t-t!" Nature cried as she grabbed the sheets.

She had never felt anything like that before. It felt so damn good and so damn powerful. She squeezed her legs tightly around Quest's neck, nearly squeezing the life out of him.

"Ohhh-h-h," she cried.

Her legs violently rumbled as her juices flowed onto the bed, and of course, all over Quest's face. He was drenched like he had stuck his head in a pool of water.

"Damn!" he whispered. "All of that for me."

Quest laughed and got up. He then grabbed a towel to wipe his face.

"Tell me you belong to me," Quest demanded as he straddled Nature.

"I belong to you, babe," Nature told him. She was stuck in a trance. Better believe that she wasn't a hostage, though. She wanted to be there.

Quest took his time with Nature. He was extra gentle since it was her first time. He wanted to make her feel as special and loved as he could.

His warm thickness filled Nature's insides, and her walls wrapped tightly around it. Quest could have cum at that moment, but he wanted to hold on for a bit and give Nature something to remember.

He licked and kissed all over her body with his thickness still deep inside of her.

Nature had explored so many things that her vagina could do. The thing she loved the best was the multiple orgasms that she was experiencing.

They shared the word love with each other so much that one would have thought they'd worn it out. But with them, that was far from the case. They truly loved each other, and words couldn't explain how they felt. The love attraction could be fatal if the two of them weren't careful...

Quest stroked Nature to oblivion. Multiple orgasms and passion marks later, she lay wrapped in his arms.

Nature stared at the wall while tucked tightly in Quest's arms. She finally felt like she belonged—like she was loved. That was a feeling she never wanted to lose. Nature wished she could just freeze that beautiful night and cherish it forever. She forever desired to live in that moment.

"Quest, I have something to tell you," Nature said while turning around and looking him in his eyes.

Quest shook his head. "Whatever it is, I don't care, Nature. The only thing I want to hear is that you love me. The rest, fuck it." He planted a wet kiss on her lips.

Nature turned back around, staring at the wall.

"I love you, Nature."

"I love you too, Quest," she replied.

He held her tightly in his arms. For years, he thought he was in love, yet, that very night, he found out the real meaning of love. When you loved, your heart danced to a different beat. The beat that his heart never danced to before, the beat that he didn't know existed.

Quest wanted to propose to Nature right there, sealing the lifetime deal. He had thought about it a few times, but it was too soon, and he didn't want her to feel like he was forcing her into anything. Since he didn't want to scare her off or anything of that sort, he decided to wait, but soon, he would make Nature his wife. He didn't mind going the extra mile to make her smile. Never in his life had he wanted to make anyone happier than he wanted to make her.

Quest closed his eyes and quietly thanked God for bringing him the woman he desired, the woman he dreamed of—the woman he spent countless nights praying for. He was a true witness that God was real, and there was power in prayer because his prayers were definitely answered.

After minutes of thanking God and hearing Nature softly snoring, he was able to peacefully drift off to sleep. Most importantly, he was happily in love with the woman wrapped tightly in his arms.

CHAPTER TEN

*T*he next day, Nature woke up with the aroma of a home-cooked breakfast lingering in the air. She stretched her arms and smiled. The first night with her lover was absolutely amazing. Quest swept her right off her feet, and she only prayed for many more nights like that. She grabbed her stomach, suddenly feeling queasy.

"Oh my." Nature sighed as she tried to figure out why her stomach was suddenly so upset.

"Please don't be one of those chicks talking about, I'm eight hours and four minutes pregnant," Quest joked while walking into the room with a tray of food.

Nature gazed at him and shook her head. "Don't try to make me out to be like your little exes," she joked.

Quest set the tray of food on the bed. He had an assortment of fruits, plain and blueberry bagels, pastries, bacon, scrambled eggs with cheese, and grits with shrimp.

"Dang, babe, all of this for me? I can't possibly eat all of this food." Nature grabbed a strip of bacon and some fruit, then started to eat them like she hadn't eaten for days.

"Damn, slow down," Quest joked.

Nature playfully nudged him.

"Quest, I don't know what to say. Your hospitality has been beyond the standards I expected. I'm just so thankful. I'm speechless. Like, damn Quest, all of this for me?"

He wrapped his arms tightly around Nature and kissed her, not caring that she had crumbs all over her mouth. He was so much in love; he would have drunk from her dirty bathwater.

"You deserve the world, and I'm going to give you exactly that. I just want you to treat me well, be loyal to me, talk to me when something is bothering you, keep it real with me, and be my best friend no matter what. I think it was our destiny to meet. God placed us together for many reasons. We want each other, and we need each other."

Nodding her head, Nature agreed with Quest. She wanted him, and she felt like she needed him. He was who she prayed for.

"What are your plans for today?" Quest quizzed.

Nature shrugged. "I really don't have much to do. I may just go home and do some laundry or something."

Hearing Nature mention going home, Quest started to feel a bit sad.

"Or you can just stay here. We can go get some movies from the Redbox, grab some good food and snacks, lay back, and spend some quality time together," Quest suggested.

Nature gave it a quick thought; she was right where she wanted to be. Quest extending that offer was a blessing. She didn't want to leave him, plus she had her little spend the night bag with extras outfits just in case.

"Well, I guess I can stay the night again," she agreed.

A WEEK HAD PASSED, and Nature was still with Quest. She didn't want to leave him, yet she didn't want to overstay her welcome.

"I really have to go home today. I have to help my mother out, plus my father misses me, and so does my best friend."

"Damn, you go home, and I'm going to miss you," Quest admitted, showcasing a sad, puppy dog look on his face.

"Awww, babe, don't act like that. I promise, let me go home, change my clothes, and check on my family, and I promise I will be back tomorrow," she told him.

"Tomorrow morning?" Quest asked.

"Tomorrow morning," Nature agreed.

Quest hated to see her leave. As soon as she left, he felt lonely. He hated that feeling more than he thought. Grabbing his cell phone, he called his best friend Ron.

"Wait, so she was real? Like a real chick, yo? Was she ugly? Too fat? Too skinny? What, she didn't have any teeth?"

Ron questioned, not believing that Quest's dream girl was actually real.

Quest grabbed his cell phone and scrolled through some pictures he had taken of himself and Nature. He stopped at his favorite one and handed Ron the phone.

"Damn, she fine! She's really real. I'ma need to check this POF thing out," Ron spoke.

"Go ahead and download that app. You won't be disappointed."

"Yeah, because ever since that trifling bitch of mine left, she's been making my life hell. It's about that time for me to move on with my life."

"Yeah, bro, move on. What you waiting for? I bet she got a new man already and doing her thing. She probably not even thinking about your ass. Some chicks don't want to see you happy if it's not with them. Bad part, they don't be even wanting your ass. They just don't want to see you with anyone else. That's why you have to say fuck it, move on, and leave the past in the past."

"Speaking of past, you wouldn't believe who I ran into the other night."

"Who?" Quest quizzed.

"Tara!"

"Awww, man." Quest grabbed a slice of pizza, "I don't want to hear about her. I'm leaving her exactly where she at —in the past. Now that is one trifling bitch I don't want to remember. Staying up in my shit with a whole another man, telling him she loves him and shit. Hell, I don't even know if

I was the side nigga or the main nigga." Quest attempted to turn his pain into a bit of laughter. It was evident that he was still pissed about how Tara had done him, especially after everything he did for her.

"Yeah, she was asking about you, saying she needed to talk to you. She said she texted you a few times, but you didn't reply."

"Man, if you ever see that bitch again, tell her I said fuck her," Quest spat.

Hearing those final words, Ron decided to drop the Tara conversation altogether.

"Yo, see if Nature has any friends for me," Ron stated.

"You know what? She does have a best friend that she's always talking about."

"That's what's up. Does she look good too?"

"I've never seen her before, but I'll put you deep. Don't be fucking shit up for me either, nigga. This is the one right here."

"I hear you." Ron got up and started grabbing his stuff. "Set up a double date for your boy. Let me get over here and pick up my son while she's still letting me see my kids."

"Alright, I will call you later."

Once Ron left, Quest started to feel a bit bored and lonely. He grabbed his cell phone to see if Nature had texted him, but she hadn't. To kill time, he decided to clean his already clean house from top to bottom.

That night, the loneliness irked his soul, especially after

spending an entire week with Nature in his arms every night.

"This is my last night alone, I promise," Quest said to himself and meant every word.

Once Nature came back, he had no intention of letting her go back home.

CHAPTER ELEVEN

*R*on smiled as she sat across from Michelle; he was definitely feeling her. He'd never dated a chocolate female before, but Michelle was about to be an exception. She was thick in all the right places, and she had big, perky breasts, just the way he liked them. She wore her long, thick natural hair. Michelle was a beautiful black goddess who matched his fly for sure.

"So, what do you like to do for fun, Michelle?" Ron questioned while licking his bottom lip.

Michelle gave him a coy smile. She knew he was flirting with her, and she didn't mind a bit. Ron's chocolate self was really attractive. In fact, the freak in her wanted to jump his bones that instant.

"I like to do a lot of things for fun. I'm a fun kind of girl, with class." Michelle winked.

Ron stared at her for a moment, wondering if Michelle was offering him an open invitation to something that he just might be interested in.

"You like whips and chains?" Ron asked.

Michelle giggled like a high school teenager.

"Oh my God, I do hope y'all know we are sitting right across from y'all," Nature teased.

"To answer your question, I like it all," Michelle flirted. "Now, if y'all will kindly excuse me, I have to go to the little girl's room." She looked at Nature and winked.

As Michelle walked away from the table, Ron had his eyes on her backside. He loved what he saw on the outside and was dying to see what the inside felt like. He gave it a minute or so before he excused himself.

"This food is upsetting my stomach. I'll be back," Ron sputtered before excusing himself.

Nature looked at Quest, and the two of them burst into a chuckle.

"See, your friend is just nasty." She smirked.

"Nah, that's not my friend. That was your nasty friend who got up and left first."

"Whatever."

RON WALKED to the men's room; he really had to use the bathroom, but afterward, he would pay Michelle a little visit. He opened the door to a pitch-black bathroom and poked his head in, looking for the light switch. Just as he was about to reach up and grab it, he was touched by the softest set of hands he had ever felt.

"You came looking for me?" Michelle whispered.

Ron couldn't see her, but he could smell the expensive perfume she wore.

"You mean you came looking for me. You in the men's room," Ron replied.

"Aww, dang, I must have gotten lost," Michelle softly said.

She grabbed Ron and pull him closer to her. In the dark, she reached for his face. Once she rubbed her hands across his lips, she leaned in for a passionate kiss.

"Damn," Ron cooed.

Michelle dropped to her knees, slowly unbuttoning his pants. She pulled out his manhood and decided she was one lucky girl. His dick was big and thick, just the way she preferred it.

"Oh, shit-t-t-t," Ron moaned, almost losing his balance and stumbling back.

Michelle was performing on him the best way she knew how. She pulled his thickness out of her mouth, slopping her tongue all over it as if she was trying to savor his unique taste.

Ron was ready to lose his mind; never in his life had his dick been sucked so good.

The slurping sounds and Ron's passionate moans were the only noises in the pitch-black bathroom.

"Oh please, please don't stop," Ron moaned as he felt himself about to reach his peak.

Michelle could feel his penis swelling inside her mouth. She thrived off having the ability to make a man cum so fast. Her head game was super official; she would put money on it that she could out-suck anyone's girlfriend or wife at that. Her dick-sucking skills were superb.

"Cum in my mouth," Michelle pulled his dick out and whispered, driving Ron insane. Seconds later, he came all in Michelle's warm mouth.

"Ahhh-h-h-h-h," he moaned. His knees were shaking so severely that he nearly fell over.

Michelle stood up, swallowing his warm semen as if the pleasure was all hers. After wiping her mouth, she grabbed Ron by the hand and pulled him toward a waiting chair in the corner.

"Sit down," she told him.

Ron sat down. He assumed she had some good pussy. There was no way her head game was that official, and the pussy wasn't. In his eyes, good head and good pussy ran together.

"Oh, yes! Is this my big dick, daddy Ron?" Michelle yelled.

She was riding the hell out of Ron, cowboy style, another one of her specialties.

Ron wrapped his arms around her waist. Leaning forward, he softly bit her back.

"Tell me whose pussy is this!" Ron squealed while reaching up and pinching her nipples.

Michelle bit her bottom lip. "This is your pussy, Ron. It's all yours," she told him.

Ron loved everything he heard. He grabbed Michelle by her waist, quickly standing her up and bending her over. Michelle grabbed his penis and shoved it right back into her.

Michelle was so tight; it didn't make any sense.

"Fuck! You are about to make me cum all in this pussy," Ron admitted. He slapped her ass so hard that it brought tears to Michelle's eyes.

"Yes, right there! Right fucking there! Right fucking there!" Ron gasped.

He gritted his teeth. Letting out a loud grunt, Ron quickly pulled himself out of Michelle and came all over her backside.

Michelle turned around and slid her tongue in his mouth. "I needed that," she softly told him. Ron couldn't see it in the dark, but Michelle was smiling from ear to ear.

She quickly searched for her little dress in the dark, then slid it back on.

"I'll see you back at the table," Michelle said before leaving him in the dark bathroom.

She rushed over to the female restroom, got herself

together, and walked back out to join her best friend and Quest.

When she sat down, they both had smiles on their faces.

"Are you okay?" Quest asked.

Michelle smiled. "I've never been better." She grabbed her drink and took a big gulp of it. "Well, I have to really get going."

She reached into her expensive handbag, grabbed a few bills out, and placed them on the table.

"Well, it's been a pleasure meeting you, Quest. You better take good care of my friend. I don't want to have to hunt you down," she joked.

"Wait. So you're going to leave before Ron comes back out?" Quest questioned.

"I'm sure he won't miss me," Michelle replied.

"Well, okay, I will call you in a few," Nature told Michelle.

She reached across the table and hugged her best friend. Nature could literally smell the aroma of dick lingering on Michelle's breath. Quest didn't know what was going on, but Nature knew her friend very well. Fucking and ducking was a game that Michelle played to see how bad a man really wanted her.

Right after Michelle left, Ron came back and sat down. At first, he thought Michelle was still in the bathroom. Then he finally asked where she was.

"Oh, you just missed her. She left already; she had an urgent matter to attend to," Nature nonchalantly stated.

"Oh, I see." Ron nodded, then grabbed his fork and stuffed his mouth with a piece of crab cake.

Deep down inside, his feelings were a bit bothered. He felt like a cheap date. Michelle had just sucked the soul out of him, then fucked the little of soul he had left and taken it with her, leaving him soulless and confused.

CHAPTER TWELVE

*N*ature grabbed her coat and slid it on. She and Quest had officially been together for five months. Things were still going well, and with her living with him, she felt like things could only get better. Since day one, Quest had been treating her like nothing less than a queen.

"Babe, you are taking all day. I'm about to grab the car. I'll beep when I get outside," Quest stated. He was standing by the front door, patiently waiting for Nature.

"I'm grabbing my coat, and I will be right down," she yelled from the top of the steps.

"Liar, liar, pants on fire. Your coat is down here," Quest yelled back while looking at Nature's coat, which was hanging on their coat hanger.

"Okay, you caught me. Here I come now," she said.

Seconds later, he heard her footsteps coming down the stairs.

"You know I could have pulled the car around," Quest said.

"No, I parked all the way around there, so I'm going to walk with you," Nature replied.

They walked out of the house, hand in hand. It was obvious that their love was still fresh; they held hands everywhere they went.

Just as they got a block away from Quest's house, he was surprised to see Tara walking their way. He thought Tara was going to say something to him, but he was even more surprised when she shot him an evil look, glared at Nature, then rolled her eyes and crossed the street.

"Why was that girl looking at me like that? Do you know her?" Nature questioned.

"Nah, I thought you knew her. But don't worry about her, babe. She's just some hating chick, mad that you look so damn good," Quest said.

A few seconds later, his phone vibrated in his pockets. Quest put money on it that it was Tara texting him.

When they got to the car, Quest walked over to the passenger side and opened the door for Nature. Once she got in, he walked behind the car and made his way to the driver's side. He stopped, and without looking at the message Tara had sent him, he put her on the blocked list.

Quest and Nature rode around the entire day, shopping and spending quality time together.

"Babe, we need to hurry up and get back home. You know Michelle will be over in a few. She's helping me press my hair for tomorrow," Nature told him.

"Right, I'm going to drop you off and then go hang out with Ron for a few," Quest said.

Michelle and Nature sat around the living room, drinking and having fun.

"WHAT HAVE you been up to, Michelle? I miss you so much." Nature took a sip of her wine.

"Nothing much, just fucking your dad," Michelle expressed and took a sip of her wine as well.

"What?" Nature said with the glass to her lips.

"I'm just joking," Michelle lied. She wanted to come clean with Nature, but it wasn't the right moment.

"Anyway, Michelle, girl, let me tell you. My man is absolutely amazing. I never in my life thought someone loving me like this was possible. He's everything I ever dreamed of and everything I ever wanted. He's really a good man, and I love him so much," Nature bragged for what seemed like the thousandth time to Michelle.

Michelle grabbed her glass again and gulped down her drink. She quickly poured herself another glass, gulping that down as well, needing to prepare herself for Nature's Quest talking. Knowing Nature, she could go on literally for hours talking about Quest.

"Whew, that was so good... Look at you, girl, glowing. I'm so glad you are finally happy. You deserve it so much, Nature."

"Michelle, I'm beyond happy!"

"Nature..." Michelle sighed. "I don't want you to think that I'm trying to rain on your parade or anything. But... does Quest know?"

The room grew eerily quiet. Nature got up and walked over to the window. She stared out of it for a few seconds with her glass of wine in her hand. As she took a few sips, tears started to slowly fall from her eyes. She cleared her throat.

"No, I didn't tell him yet. I don't know how I can tell him. The last thing I want to do is break his heart, Michelle. He's been through so much already. Trust me, keeping the truth from him hurts so bad. Every time my man mentions having kids, it breaks my heart into so many pieces. It's like I finally got what I prayed for, and I'm not ready to lose him. It may seem selfish, but Michelle, I can't lose him."

Michelle felt so bad for her friend. She walked over to Nature and ran her hands through her hair, then flipped her hair to the back of her head. "I know how much you love him. And before this goes too far, I really think you should tell him the truth. Everything that happens in the dark will one day surface to the light. It will be so much better coming from you than anyone else," Michelle exclaimed.

"I know, I know, Michelle. I just don't want to lose him. I love him so much," Nature cried. She rested her head on Michelle's shoulder and cried her eyes out.

QUEST SAT on the edge of the bed, waiting for Nature to get dressed. She had been in the bathroom for over two hours. He didn't know what she was doing in there, but he patiently waited for her.

Nature's phone vibrated, and he glanced over at it. Quest walked over to the nightstand and picked it up. Part of him wanted to go through her cell phone; after Tara, he had trust issues. Deciding against it, he walked over to the bathroom and went to turn the knob, but it was locked.

"Nature, what is taking you so long? You said your parents are expecting us at five."

Nature unlocked the door and opened it with her makeup brush in her hand. "Babe, you know you can't rush perfection. I'm in here beating my face to the gawds! Give me a few more minutes. I swear I'm always running behind. My mother knows I'll be late for my own funeral. She said so herself."

Quest heard a knock at their front door. "That's Ron at the door."

"Okay, go ahead and get it. I'll be down in a few more minutes," Nature replied.

"I swear you better hurry up." Quest smirked. "What's up, Ron?" he yapped while opening the front door.

"Man, just chilling, chilling. Thank you for the loan. Ever since Monique left with the kids, then put me on child support with her trifling ass, this shit has been killing me." Ron reached into his pocket and handed Quest back the four hundred dollars that he borrowed from him.

"No need to explain anything to me. You're good for it."

Quest reached in his pocket and pulled out a ring box. He opened it to show Ron.

"Damn, you're really ready to settle down?" Ron questioned.

"Yeah, man, she's the one. I'm ready to make her my wife, have a family with her and live happily ever after," Quest admitted.

"That's some deep shit, man. I ain't going to lie. When you first was on that dating app and started talking to Nature, I thought that shit was a joke. I was kind of skeptical because it's so many imposters on there. Nature's a little weird at times; I can't put my finger on it. But that's none of my business either. I'm a little salty about how her friend got some of this good dick, and I never heard from her nor saw her again. But I'm happy for you, man. You lucked up, so shoot your shot before it's too late. You have my blessing."

"Yeah, I lucked up for sure."

"Now that you are off the market, you should—"

Nature walked in, interrupting Quest and Ron's conversation. Quest quickly put the ring back into his pocket.

"Hi, Ron," Nature spoke.

"Hey, Nature. I was just about to get out of here. I will hit you up later, Quest," Ron said and quickly excused himself.

CHAPTER THIRTEEN

$\mathcal{N}$ature and Quest stood at the front door of Nature's parents' condo. Once she moved in with Quest, she gave them her key back. She was certain that she would never return home. Nature had planned a lifetime commitment with her man.

She brushed the lint off Quest's shirt. "I'm so happy for you to meet my parents. I know they are going to love you, babe."

"Yeah, I hope so," Quest replied.

He was a bit nervous about meeting Nature's family. He hoped they would really like him and wouldn't come between him and Nature. Sometimes parents could get in the way, and that was the last thing he wanted.

Nature knocked at the door again. "Mom, Dad. What are y'all doing? It's me."

Michelle walked to the door and opened it. Nature was surprised to see her there.

"Girl, what are you doing here?"

"Well, hey to you too! Hey, Quest! Mom and Dad are already at the table, waiting on your slow behind. We are hungry, so hurry up and get in here."

"Michelle, what are you doing here? Every time someone says something about food, your greedy ass don't miss out. Damn, girl."

"Girl, stop trying to play me like that. And stop with all that complaining. For your information, Mom called me over this morning to do her hair. When she told me you were coming, I decided to stick around to see your ugly ass! Besides, you know I wasn't about to turn down any collard greens or neckbones."

"Whatever." Nature laughed while placing her coat on the stool next to the door.

Quest took his coat off, and Nature set it on top of hers.

She grabbed his hand, and the two of them walked into the living room together.

Quest didn't know that he was about to walk into a big surprise—a blast from the past.

When he walked in and saw Veronica, he was speechless.

Veronica was on her cell phone, and she quickly ended her call. Standing up from her seat, she was more than speechless.

"Wait. Quest, what are you doing here?" Veronica questioned, confused as hell.

"Mom... wait, you know him?"

Sam quickly jumped up. Quest was a young, handsome man, and he wanted to know exactly how his wife knew him too.

"Yeah, you know him, Veronica?" Sam questioned.

Veronica looked at Sam and rolled her eyes. Their marriage was far from perfect, but marriage was a business as far as she was concerned. She was benefiting from it and had no plans to let her cash cow go. She knew all about Sam and Michelle. For that reason, she wouldn't dare let her husband ever lay a finger on her, with his trifling, sick ass.

Deep down inside, she hated his guts; she couldn't stand him. There were plenty of nights that she wished he would die in his sleep, so she could reap his benefits and at least draw a monthly social security check off him. With the four life insurance policies she had on him, she would be financially straight and even happier with him dead.

"In fact, I do know him, Nature. If you hadn't been so secretive, you would have known that I knew him," Veronica spat.

Sam was annoyed and very frustrated. "Exactly how do you know him, Veronica?" he sternly spat.

Veronica looked at Sam and rolled her eyes again. "Sam, would you shut the hell up? That's neither here nor there. Damn, you are getting on my mother fucking nerves already!" Veronica fussed.

"Veronica, this is your daughter?" Quest asked. His mind raced back to his conversations with Veronica, his last conversation at that. Veronica always mentioned a son yet never said anything about a daughter.

Veronica looked at Nature, shooting her the evil eye. "What the hell is going on here?" she hissed.

Michelle grabbed her drink off the table and took a few sips. "Mmm hmm, I told you. You should have told him," she whispered.

Veronica was annoyed by Sam and now by her child. She was pissed that somehow Nature had landed on the good dick that she had hopped off, trying to be a good wife for the time being.

Nature stood there, nearly in tears.

"Know what? What the hell is going on here? What she knew about me this entire time? You set me up with her?" Quest questioned; he was so confused.

Veronica's eyes moved to a family portrait on the wall. The entire time, Quest had no clue that the truth resided on the walls around him.

He followed Veronica's eyes to the portrait. When he stepped closer, his body instantly flushed with unbearable hurt.

"Oh, hell no! What the fuck is this? What type of sick shit is this, yo!" he yelled.

Quest turned around and rushed to the front door. He snatched his coat off the chair.

"Wait, Quest!" Nature ran behind him.

Quest allowed the door to slam in her face. He was so furious—all he wanted to do was get far away from Nature and her family.

"Wait, Quest, please. Please let me explain," Nature yelled as she ran behind him.

She was angry, remorseful, and devastated—her emotions were all over the place. Nature could admit that she was wrong. She wanted to be honest with Quest, but the fear of losing him was too intense, and she just couldn't.

Quest stopped in his tracks. Heated was an understatement. "Explain what? How the fuck are you going to explain that you are a fucking man, bitch! Nigga, I should beat our ass into a mother fucking coma right now! Back the hell away from me now! You are dead ass wrong, and you are sick. Mother fuckers get killed for shit like this!" Quest hollered at the top of his lungs. He was so furious that saliva flew from his mouth as he yelled.

Nature fearfully jumped; she was shaking in her boots. At that moment, she was afraid of Quest. This was the first time she had seen him so upset, especially with her. She felt like she had failed him.

Nature broke down and cried. "What about love? What about the way we made each other feel? What about Nature's Quest? We can't help who we are, and we can't help who we love. Quest, please..." she cried her heart out.

Quest wasn't trying to hear it as he balled his fist, seconds away from beating Nature's ass. "You are fucking sick, Nature. You are dead wrong for this shit! I better not ever see you again, or you are a dead man, woman, it! Or whatever the fuck you are!"

Nature hated to see Quest go. Deep in her heart, she knew that what she had with Quest was over for good. How could he ever forgive her? Was he really supposed to forgive her after she tricked him by not telling him that she was born a male and not the woman he fell in love with?

Even before her sex change, she had tricked him by not telling him that he was having phone sex with a man who had a dick that was bigger than his. Guilt consumed Nature —all she wanted at that moment was for someone to understand her...

She walked back into the house to face the music with her parents.

"See, I told you, Nature. You were supposed to be transparent at all times. Had you been honest, none of this would've happened. So, wipe them damn tears and get your shit together now," Veronica told Nature. She'd had one too many drinks, and she was furious that Michelle and Sam were acting like she didn't know they were fucking behind her back.

"Mom, I loved him. I really loved him, and I know he loved me too!" Nature cried.

Sam shook his head; he was tired of all the bullshit.

"You know what? Fuck this shit. I'm not about to sit around and feel sorry for you. Do you know how many people have lost their lives for shit like this or almost lost their lives? Suppose that man found out some other way and killed your ass? This shit has to stop. I'm not ready to lose my son over some gender crisis bullshit."

Although Veronica was mad at Nature, she wasn't about to allow Sam to speak to Nature so harshly.

"Okay, Sam, you are out of line. That's enough!" Veronica argued.

"You know what, Veronica? Shut the fuck up! You are the one to blame for this shit. You was the bitch who took my son from me. Telling him that boys can be princesses too at eight years old, painting his nails while I was at work, letting him put wigs and shit on. Bitch, you are the one who stole my child from me. Every time I tried to discipline our son, you would stop me. You always said I was too hard on him. You babied him and made him believe he was someone who he could never be. You are the one to blame. And because of you, we could have lost our son Nathaniel tonight."

"Enough, Daddy! Enough! And for the record, Nathaniel is dead, and if you can't address me as Nature, then you can forget about me. I am who I am."

"You are fucking confused! You can never be a woman, Nathaniel. You'll never be a woman or even have the authentic experience that a woman has. You won't experience menstrual cycles, and you won't know what it feels like to bear a child. Hell, on your license, it says that you are a man. You'll never be able to change that." Sam kept throwing salt on the already open wound. He had so much on his chest that he had been holding in for so long.

Veronica walked over to the window, and tears started to stream from her eyes. Sam was right; she was the one to blame for what Nature had done to herself. She was the creator of the entire chaos. When Veronica found out she was pregnant, she was sure that she would get the daughter she'd always prayed for. Once she found out she was having a boy, she was devastated. She wanted to abort the child and try again. Her dream was to have a daughter to go shopping with, get their hair done together, go on spa dates, talk about boys, and all those things.

She burst out crying so hard that she began to shake. The room was filled was so many hurt souls and uncontrolled emotions.

Sam sat down and huffed; he was a father who had been cheated out of a son. He had every right to have resentment toward his wife.

"I'm sorry. I'm sorry, I can't help who I am!" Nature cried.

Michelle was lost for words. She slowly got up and walked over to Nature. She wrapped her arms around Nature tightly, allowing her to cry her soul out in her arms.

"It's okay, Nature. I understand. You are right, we can't help who we are, and we can't help who we love. We are unique and beautiful, no matter if the world thinks otherwise. We are strong unicorns, and we shall get over all this hurt and pain together. Things are going to get so much better. There are people out there who will accept us and love us for who we are. Trust me, everyone can't handle who we are; some only know how to hurt us. I been through this before, and I know exactly how you feel," Michelle spoke while shooting an evil eye at Sam.

Sam stared at Michelle while shaking his head.

"You know what? I need to get some fresh air," Veronica stated. She snatched her cell phone off the table, grabbed her coat and keys, and left without another word to anyone.

Sam got up and quietly walked to their bedroom.

"I'm going to go use the bathroom, and we are going to drink some wine, eat this good food, and have a little girls' night," Michelle stated, trying to cheer her friend up.

As soon as Michelle walked away, Nature rushed to the front door. Her mind was made up. She was going to fight for what and who she loved.

QUEST HAD GONE through two bottles of liquor. He was confused, hurt, pissed off, and a mixture of so many different emotions. He felt like he had been fucked; betrayed in the worst way. Again, he had fallen for someone, and they had played him. Made him out to be a fool again. What disturbed him even worse was that he was starting to question his own sexuality.

"A fucking man! A fucking man!" Quest cried as he paced his living room floor. "A fucking man!" he hollered.

Quest picked up an empty liquor bottle and looked into the tiny hole for more alcohol. He was already past his limit, but he didn't care. His idea was to get drunk as a skunk, so drunk that he would forget every damn thing that was on his mind.

He walked over to his candles and began to light them. In the process, he started kicking and throwing things all over the place. He had already destroyed his entire house. He kicked over a box, and his gun fell out. Quest looked at the gun like it was an award. Slowly, he picked it up as tears of pain fell from his eyes and snot smeared all over the place.

"A fucking man!" he cried.

Quest's hands began to shake as he pondered whether he should blow his own brains out. The way he felt, he didn't think it was possible to live with himself anymore. Sliding down to the floor, he grabbed his cell phone and thought about Tara. Although she was a lying, cheating ass bitch, she always knew how to cheer him up.

He scrolled to her name and clicked on the messages. His hands shook as he read the message: *Quest, I know you probably hate me, and I'm the last person you want to hear from. But, Quest, that person I saw you with the other day... I don't know how to say this... But that's an old classmate of mine. He's a boy, and his name is Nathaniel. I'm so sorry. I don't know if you are now into those types of people. I remember conversations that we used to have about transgender, and you weren't too transgender friendly... Call me if you need me.*

"Ahh-h-h-h!" Quest roared. He threw an empty glass at

the wall, and it shattered. Tara knew before him. How did he not know that he was sleeping with a man?

Then he thought about Michelle, and his mind went back to the details Ron had shared about them fucking in the dark and how tight her pussy was. Her leaving and never mentioning Ron again. When it happened, he thought it was peculiar but didn't waste much time thinking about it. He remembered how big Michelle's feet and hands were—the strong, manly features were as clear as day now. How did he overlook that shit back then? He was disgusted with himself even more. Quest couldn't imagine telling Ron that he slept with a man. Ron would most likely blame him, find Michelle, and kill her.

"Why me? What the hell did I do to deserve this shit?" Quest cried.

Quest stood up, stumbling over everything he threw on the floor. His vision was blurred as he grabbed his cell phone and turned on his radio. Seconds later, all the speakers that lined the walls in his home began to blare lyrics that didn't do any justice to his already hurting soul.

"I been on the low. I been taking my time. I feel like I'm out of my mind. It feels like my life isn't mine. I been on the low. I been taking my time. I feel like I'm out of my mind. It feels like my life isn't mine. I don't want to be alive, I don't want to be alive, I just want to die. I just want to die today. I just don't want to be alive; I just want to die-e-e-e-e," Quest sang. He spun in circles with the gun in his hand. "I just want to die, I just want to die today," he chanted. His mind was elsewhere.

Right in his living room, he transformed into someone he didn't even recognize. Love was immensely powerful; it could change you completely.

NATURE STOOD outside the house she shared with Quest. She looked up at the home with tears in her eyes; the place was pitch dark. Sighing deeply, she gazed down at her cell phone. Michelle had been calling her repeatedly since she'd left. She turned her cell phone off. Part of her said to leave and go back to her parents' house. Yet, the other part, the other part... was telling her to fight for what she loved.

Her hands violently shook as she stuck her key into the door. She walked into the house and saw stuff thrown all over the place. Gazing down the hallway, she noticed candles placed around the room as music blared through the speakers. Over the music, she could hear Quest crying.

It broke her heart into a million pieces. She was shaking so badly as she slowly walked down the hall, stuck in a trance.

Nature stopped at the door frame and watched as Quest cried his eyes out. She hated herself for causing him such agony. His pain was palpable. It ran through Nature's body, sending chills all over.

"Quest." She shivered.

Quest looked up and stared at Nature. He didn't know if his mind was fucking with him or what. When Nature walked over and wrapped her arms around him, it brought him to reality a bit.

"Quest, I know you felt like I used you. I know I'm wrong, and it hurts me that I hurt you so bad. I hate that I fell in love with you and wasn't honest!" Nature cried.

Quest wrapped his arms tightly around Nature. The two of them sat and cried for a few minutes. They were connected by more than love; their souls were literally tied to each other. No one would ever understand the love they shared. Quest wanted to hate Nature, yet he couldn't. Even after finding out her true identity, he still couldn't help but love her. But what mattered was that he hated himself for blindly falling for someone who wasn't honest with him.

Quest reached in his pocket and pulled out the ring. He had been waiting to get on his knee and ask Nature to be his wife after he got the blessing of her father and mother.

Nature cried even harder when Quest slid the ring onto her ring finger.

"I loved you, Nature. I loved you so damn much that my heart obtained this special beat just for you. I would have followed you to the moon and back. I would have followed you to the end of this earth. You meant everything to me, but you made me feel so small, so worthless," Quest admitted.

He was fighting an undefeated battle of fatal love. Too fatal for either of them.

"I love you, Nature!" Quest cried.

"I love you too, Quest. I love you so much," Nature responded.

Quest grabbed her face with his left hand and leaned toward her. They were forehead to forehead as they stared deeply into each other's eyes—piercing their souls.

"I love you," Quest softly whispered.

Nature felt something, a feeling that she had to accept.

Quest lifted his right hand, displaying the gun he was holding. Nature was so scared, yet she didn't move. She cried even harder. Quest slowly pushed the gun to her face. He moved it to her mouth and placed the barrel between her teeth.

Nature's tears fell all over the gun—she began to shake uncontrollably as she stared at Quest. If loving him was going to cost her life, then so be it. She knew that she would die in the name of love, and she'd much rather die by the hands of a man who truly loved her, and she loved him back.

She swallowed the forbidden lump that formed in her throat. Quest was worth way more than the trust. She just wished that she would have been honest with him from day one. She hated how much she hurt him, and now she had to settle with the truth setting her free. *I love you, Quest. I love you with everything in my heart. I love you so much. I will forever love you. Please forgive me,* she expressed.

Flashes of her mother, her father, and Michelle ran through her mind. She wondered what they would do without her. How her deadly decisions would affect her family. Repetitive rapid thoughts raced through her mind. Her mother told her to be transparent at all times. She wished she would have listened. Yet, it felt so damn good to finally be loved by someone than to never be loved by anyone. Was it that bad that she wanted to be loved for once in her life, even though Quest fell in love with someone she wasn't? He fell in love with a lie.

BAM! The gun went off.

"I love you! I love you!" Quest cried. He turned the gun on himself without a second thought.

BAM! The gun went off; blood and brain matter splashed his walls, and his dead body fell right on top of his lover's...

"Be true to yourself, and most importantly, be true to the ones you love and the ones who love you. You deserve the truth, and so do they..." - Angel Williams

SNEAK PEEK: HOEISM AND MATRIMONY

Bouns

We were riding the street and my mother kept nagging and bitching for no reason. I felt like she always did these sort of things just to get under my skin. Before we left the house she told me to grab her damn purse, simply because it was 'her' purse. I purposely left it sitting on the couch where she last had it. Then when we get twenty minutes away from home I asked her could we stop at Burger King so I could be. Oh gosh you would have thought I asked her to drive to me Mexico the way she was throwing a fit. That was my mother though she was stuck in her own ways, had it be Tesa she wouldn't damn near killed us trying to pull over to the nearest place for her pretty pretty little princess to release her bladder. Tesa is my sister and I truly love her to death but I despise her at times.

The relationship she has with my mother makes me envious of her, she was always the favorite and no matter what I would do my mother would never show me favoritism. So with that being said, I decided to take a little revenge in my own hands. Call me vindictive but I look at it as vengeance being mines. No vindictive intended, I just woke up on the wrong side of the bed with a little hell in me.

"Every damn time we go someone where Lisa you have to use the bathroom or you forget something back at home! I don't understand why you just can't be more like Tesa." My mother screamed at me. She didn't know how much she irked my soul and how bad it hurt for her to compare me to Tesa. I glanced over at Tesa who was sitting inches away from me smiling. She got a kick out of my mother always putting her on a pedal stool like she was a queen or something. Tesa! Tesa! Tesa! I got tired of my mother ranting. "You should have just left me at home with daddy." I whined. The mention of my dad sent my mother over the edge. "Don't tell me what I should have done!" She yelled, slamming down on the breaks causing us all to jerk forward. I hit my head on the back of her seat, I touched my mouth to assure that I wasn't bleeding from the mouth. My father and her had been arguing the night before for hours. She yelled and screamed at my father all night. He couldn't get a break even if his life had depended on it. He went to the kitchen my mother was walking behind him arguing, he went into the bedroom and she was right behind him and even if he tried to go hide out in the bathroom that was impossible, she was on his ass like white on rice. My mother was accusing my father of cheating on her in revenge from when she got caught having in affair two years ago. She swore up and down that it was another woman in his life. But she was totally wrong... If she couldn't read between the lines then she was damn fool!

She turned around and stared me in the eyes. "Look here you little hell raiser! Don't get under my skin today." She grimaced. She then turned around and pressed down on the gas, we were going so fast I nearly caught a whiplash from my window that was rolled down. A devious smile crept across my face as we pulled up into our driveway. "Now go use the bathroom and get my damn purse!" My mother told me throwing the car in park. I knew how to agitate her, I slowly climbed out the car, I looked across the street and noticed the familiar red truck parked across the street as it was always parked across the street when we left on outings. Every Monday, Wednesday and Friday night my father would give my mother an allowance to take us out and do whatever she wanted with the money. She was a stay at home mother and truthfully I believed if she didn't have kids she still wouldn't carry her ass to work. So every time that allowance was given to her she would take us out, sometimes she would just let us tag along with her while she went to the mall to get pampered and shop. It had been many occasions where she would buy Tesa something and wouldn't buy me anything. None of that mattered though because when I told my father he would take me out and spend a father and daughter day with me. "Uh huh!" She grunted and jumped out the car. "I have to use the bathroom too." Tesa said and got out the car behind us. My mother turned the key and opened the door and I swear she had to smell it, because I could smell it and clearly Tesa could smell of fresh sex and booty-tang lingering through the air. My mother held her nose up in the air and starting sniffling like a hound dog, sniffling right to the trail of her cheating ass husband. "Deeper! Deeper! Ohh-h-h-h deeper Tyrone." We heard a voice cry out. Tesa covered her mouth and I had to too to hold in the laughter.The banging against the floor was so obnoxious and powerful it felt like daddy was about to knock the roof off the ceiling. "What's that sound mommy?" Tesa had the audacity to ask as if she wasn't well familiar with that sound.

My mother quickly rushed towards the closet and grabbed a golf club out of it. She was vexed, the look on her face was priceless. "You two stay right here!" My mother pointed her finger at us. Tesa and I didn't care what she was saying, wanting to find out who back daddy was banging out we followed right behind her. Well it was nothing new to me because this wasn't going to be the first time I caught my father. But it was definitely all new to my mother and Tesa.

Tesa and I both jotted upstairs, my mother ran to the bedroom door and without hesitation she snatched it open. We all were in for a surprised..."Oh my." My mother cried out covering her mouth. She was so devastated, lost and confused that she became speechless. Finally something shut up nagging Nancy! I wasn't only surprised because the position I caught my daddy in, I thought he would have at least been man enough to take over! But that wasn't the case. "Daddy!" Tesa screamed. My mother grabbed he chest, deep breaths escaped. She fell back against the wall and looked as if she was about to have a heart attack. The golf club hung freely on her right side. "Uh——-" She tried to speak but couldn't prepared her words. I bet all sorts of thoughts were running through her mind. "What the hell is this shit Tyrone?" My mother screamed. My father was bent over and getting all the glory one could get with a penis rammed up his rectum. Not that it was just any penis, it was my God father's penis. I smiled, "Hi daddy, hi uncle Steven." My mother looked at me with pure disgust on her face. I didn't care because my father was my father and I could never judge him for he loved. Hadn't my mother been such a weak ass, nagging ass bitch she wouldn't have ran my father to the next man. Had she been on top of her A game and left me the hell alone she would have noticed that every time we left the house that my God father would be just leaving when we came back. Boy if she didn't know that her shit stunk she sure as hell smelt it that day and it wasn't the booty in the air either. My God father backed up and tucked slid his boxers up. "Hey Nancy, hey Tesa, hey Lisa." He embarrassedly waived at us. "Don't you dare fucking hey me, you disgusting peace of shit!" She ranted. I burst out laughing. The nerve of her to ever call anyone disgusting. She turned her head towards me. "You little disgusting runt, I guess you see'll the humor all in this being that you go around kissing on little girls!" She grimaced. I smiled at her and shrugged my shoulders. I only got caught kissing a girl once and my mother made such a big deal out of it. Had she caught me before hand she would have caught us doing more than kissing if you catch my drift. "Like father like fucking daughter!" My mother yelled. "Tyrone what is this shit!" She yelled. I folded my arms across my shoulders, like really how was she going to ask him what was anything when the damn proof was right in front of her eyes. And she knew damn well that her eyes wasn't deceiving her. My father stood up, "I don't know what to say Nancy." He said. He grabbed the blankets from off the bed and covered himself up. "You don't know what to say?" My mother mocked him. She ran towards my father with the golf club and Whap! She swung freely, knocking him upside his head. My father took that hit like a pro. She went to swing again. "You disgusting piece of shit!" She yelled all types of verbal assaults at him. She hit him again, knocking the wind out of him. He fell backwards when he got up there was blood dripping from his face. I felt so damn bad for my father. My God father stepped forwarding defending my father, "Enough is enough Nancy!" Steven yelled her, throwing his hands up in the air. My mother looked him up and down evilly like he was scum. "You don't tell me shit, you butt fucker!" She yelled at him. Spitting venom at the two of them she was a rampage. Literally my mother was the kettle calling the pot black, she acted as if my father and her never shared a woman. I didn't understand why she thought what she did there was no wrong in it. Steven man handled her, he reached for the golf club as she swung it at him. Yanking it from her, he accidentally pushed her on the bed. "Ahhh." My mother screamed. "How are you going to let him touch your wife like this." My mother tried to exaggerate the harmlessly fall onto the bed something bigger than what it was. My father shook his head, holding his hand up to where the blood was leaking at from his head. The room was in an uproar. My mother jumped from the bed and went charging at Steven. She ran right into his hard chest. He bent her up like she was some ole filmsy doll and tossed her butt across the room. "Eukkk." She grunted. She jumped back on her feet again and this time charged at my father. "How can you do this to me!" She cried. My father poked his chest out like a man and allowed my mother to beat on him, all until she started punching him in the face. "Daddy I hate you!" Tesa charged at him and started beating him as well. I couldn't stand by and allow them to beat on my father. Yes he was wrong for cheating, especially cheating in the home that him and my mother shared. Cheating in the bed that him and my mother shared and use to make love in. That was wrong but as far as him being with Steven that was his prerogative. I loved my father and I could never judge him for who he wanted to be. "Tyrone you need to fix this. I'm out of here." Steven announced, he grabbed his pants and put them on and grabbed his shirt and got it on and got out of there within a blink of an eye. I rushed towards my mother and Tesa, who was literally beating the crap out of my father. "Stop it!" I yelled at the two of them. I was knocked Tesa off my father and pushed her to the ground. She got back up swinging at me like I was a stranger to her, trying to knock my head off. I didn't want to fight Tesa, so I kindly shoved her to the ground again. "Stop Tesa. I'm not trying to fight you." I warned her. She looked up at me from the ground and stuck her middle finger up at me. My mother rushed to my father's closet, "Get your queer ass out of here!" She yelled, yanking his stuff from the closet. She grabbed a handful and threw it outside the window. She went back for more and did the same. I looked at my father and I felt like crap for setting him up to get caught. I honestly just wanted to hurt my mother, not realizing that I was going to hurt my father even more in the long wrong. I wrapped my arms around him. "I love you no matter what daddy." I told him and kissed him on the cheeks. Tesa stared at the two of us with pure evilness in her eyes. "Of course you'll love him no matter what, you're much as a queer as he is too. You damn weirdos belong together." She yelled. She took off running out the room. My mother was still ranting and acting a fool. Tesa came back with a handful of clothing and started tossing them out of the window. I looked at them and noticed that the belongings belonged to me. I ran over towards her and before I knew it I had her hanging out of the window, over

15 feet high in the air begging for her life. "Let her go Lisa. Please let her go." My mother begged me. My sister was crying and pleading for her life. I stared into her big brown eyes and seen no type of worthiness in them. She was indeed my mothers child, she followed everything my mother did and she had all of my mother's terrible ways. "Lisa, please let your sister go before you end up really hurting her. You two are sisters and I don't want you two fighting." My father's calm voice brought me back to reality. "Let her go." I said, taunting Tesa I acted as if I was going to let her go. "No, no! Please just bring her back in the window." My mother screamed. I looked over my shoulders at my father. "Let her go?" I asked again. Our eyes locked and I swear it was like he was telling me to let her go. I grabbed Tesa and started to pull her back towards me and suddenly she started swinging at me. Causing me to lose my grip of her and before I knew it she slipped right out of my hands. "Mommy!" She yelled on top of her lungs. My father quickly reached over me and with his strong manly arms he grabbed Tesa, saving her life. Once Tesa was secured and safe my mother started snapping again. "Get your filthy hands off my child!" She screamed at my father slapping him across his hands like a disobedient toddler. Tesa sat on the bed, she was breathing hard, her chest heavily moved up and down. I know her life had just flashed right before her eyes because it sure as hell flashed right before my eyes. "You almost killed my daughter." My mother started to fuss at me. "It was an accident!" I said in defense. My father

started to get dress, I know he was fed up because I definitely was. "Where do you think you are going? You have some explaining to do!" My mother fussed at him. He shook his head and continued to get dress. Once he got done he grabbed his car keys. My mother tried to slap them out of his hands but he pushed her onto the bed. My father left out the house and harshly slammed the front door behind him. Before my mother dug all in my butt, I quickly dismissed myself, leaving her and Tesa miserable behinds alone. I went into my room and locked the door and turned my music on. Even over top of my music I could still hear my mother's annoying voice. She was beyond hurt, she had every right to be but at that moment I couldn't understand her pain because for one I was too young and for two I never experienced a heartbreak before to understand how devastating it was. I climbed into my bed and got under the covers, in a matter of minutes I was fighting my sleep until eventually sleep claimed me. I woke up and I noticed that it was still light outside. I got up and walked out of my room. The entire hallway was a mess. I walked down the steps and walked into the kitchen to get something to drink. Then I heard all of the chaos going on outside. While sipping my drink, I seen my mother from the kitchen window outside acting a fool, with her sidekick Tesa almost attached to her hip. "My husband like men!" My mother yelled on a bullhorn to whoever rode pass on our block and would give her the time of the day. I looked out on the lawn and it seemed like my father's entire life was out there. We lived in a predominately caucasian neighborhood and because we were the only african american family on the block my mother always told us to be on our best behavior, never to try to fit in but definitely not to be ignorant and do any sort of ignorance and stand out. Yet there she was outside acting like she didn't have no home training while she told everyone's my father business. Of course there was a few old nosey no lives having neighbors who stopped and got all the free scoop they could get. Anyone that was willing to listen to my mother she was willing to tell them all the bad things she could think of about my father. I shook my head and really felt awful for the shame I had brought onto my father. In the mist of my mother bashing my father I seen his Creme color Audi pulling into the driveway. "There he is! The cheating husband." My mother announced as if the paparazzi and media was out there to get all of the latest scoop. I went to the front door and I couldn't believe the signs that I seen that dressed out front yard. I walked outside to read some of them of the embarrassment my mother had nailed into our grass, attached to a poster. 'My husband is a cheater. My husband like men. Beware of the booty licker.' And many other type of crucial things in the front yard. Some of my neighbors were so intrigued with my mother's drama they were even out there taking pictures and recording the madness. My father got out of his car and did a walk of shame as he walked up the pathway that led to our home. His eyes and my mother's eyes locked with one another and in both of their eyes it was murder they wrote!

"Get your ass in this house now. I work too damn hard to have you out here carrying on like this." My father grimaced. My mother threw her hands on her hips and shifted her weight from on leg to the other. "Boy. Shut up! You can no longer tell me what to do. Maybe if you was a man I wouldn't be out here carrying on like this." My mother shot back at him. "My husband wants me to go in the house because he's embarrassed of what he has done." My mother yelled to the audience that she had. My father swept her off her feet and threw her over his shoulders. My mother was boney as heck. She stood about 5'1 and weighed a good hundred and ten pounds soak and wet. "Put me down!" My mother fussed and kicked my father as he carried her into the house. We ran in the house behind them, leaving our neighbors outside to piece rest of our business together. "You think you are going to get away with this. You are wrong, it's going to be hell for you from here and out." My mother pointed her hand in my father's face and threatened him. My father looked at her and burst out laughing, he pushed her to the side and walked off into the kitchen. "What do you mean? These past four years with you have been nothing but hell with you." He laughed. He grabbed his Colt 45 from out of the refrigerator and opened it up. He walked over to the couch, the tension in the room grew thicker by the second. My mother stood with her hands on her hips and mean mugged him and rolled her eyes at him. "You make me so sick I just want to vomit all over you." She told me my father. Tears started to parade down her cheeks. "How could you do me like this? Why couldn't you just tell me that you were no longer in love with me? Why couldn't you just tell me that you were into men and no longer attracted by me? Why did you have to humiliate me like this. I would have rather caught you in bed with my damn mother before I caught you in bed with another man!" My mother cried. She dropped to her knees grabbing her chest and bellowed a loud heart wrecking cry. "Why-y-y-y-y" Her loud voice carried throughout the house. Tesa ran over to me and wrapped her arms around me. The mood in our home just wasn't at its best. Tears ran down my cheeks as I stared at my parents. My father fingered his chin hair, the look in his eyes you could tell that he was hurting too. Then the tears slowly started to dance down his face. "Nancy I'm sorry. Trust me every day I beat myself up for what I have done. I don't know what to say, I'm merely ashamed for what I done to my family." My father admitted. I was really full of regrets, I prayed that someway somehow my father could be rehabilitated and someway my mother and he could come to some sort of understanding. "How could you do this Tyrone?" My mother stood up screaming. "How could you do this to ME! To your kids, to your family!" She yelled while beating against her chest like a wild ape. "Everything we worked so hard to build, you tore it down with your infidelity and your lies! You left us to sink all because you wanted your cake and to eat it too." My mother cried. She stormed over to him and got all up in his face. "You fucked up and you fucked us over!" She hollered while drilling her finger in his chest. She started mugging him in the face and slapping him across his face. Using him as a punching bag to release all her anger her slaps turned in harsh punches as if she was trying to knock him out. My father stood up and Wissph! He knocked my mother off of him. She fell onto of the over shake and glass made coffee table. I doubt it was her weight, it was more likely the force from my father to cause the table to shatter. "Ahhhh." My mother whimpered. She grabbed a piece of the broken glass and darted towards my father, she raised her hand and sliced him across his face. "Ahh." He screamed out in agony. My mother was out for blood, she jabbed my father again, that time in his arm and started going crazy trying to stab him to death. My father charged at her and pushed her against the wall. He wrapped his strong hand around my mother's neck and began choking her while banging her head into the floor, he sent punches across her face. I ran up to them. "Daddy!" I yelled. My father stopped and looked at me, my mother crawled from underneath him and went to the corner on the opposite side room for safety. "You two go to your rooms now!" My father screamed at Tesa and I. But either of the two of us budged, we stood there looking at my father. "Now!" He roared. Tesa and I scattered like roaches exposed to some Raid.

BOUNS

I was in my room laying across my bed and plunged my ear buds into my ear trying to tune out my mother and father arguing. They had been arguing non stop and fighting for hours. Tesa and I was forbidden to step foot outside of our rooms. I didn't know what was going to happen with my mother and father but I knew for sure they were over for good. The way they looked at one another it was with pure hatred. My mother hated my father for what he did and I believe my father blamed some of his behavior on my mother. I didn't think it was possible for a woman to push a man into the arms of another man but anything was possible. I had caught my father and my God father Steven in the same bedroom and I heard moans escaping from the room months ago when one day my mother and I got into an argument and I got out of the car and walked back home. We weren't even gone for a half an hour before my God father had arrived. Walking up to the house I seen his red Dodge Ram parked outside. I didn't think nothing of it until I got inside of the house, I went to the kitchen to get something to drink and as I put the cup to my mouth I heard the moans. I walked upstairs and placed my ears to my father's bedroom door and I could hear the sounds of two grown men moaning and groaning. I didn't know what to think of the situation. I loved my father so much I didn't want to ever betray him so I never told my mother. When she kept treating me unfair, my intentions were only to hurt her, not expose my father. But I guess things didn't turn out as I planned and I did more than expose him. My hateful decisions now could have possibly cost me a father. I overheard my mother threatening him and telling him that she was going to prohibit him from seeing us. Without my father I couldn't even began to imagine that. My father was my father and he was my best friend. When no one else had my back he would have my back for sure without any questions asked. My mother should have known something was going on with my father. Before I caught him I even noticed something was wrong with their relationship. I barely seen him walking up behind her and wrapping his arms around her waist and kissing all over her neck. I barely heard them having sex on the late night when they thought Tesa and I were sleep. I couldn't even recall the last time I heard my mother screaming "Tyrone!" on the top of her lungs. And not to mention my mother had kicked my father out of the bedroom hat their shares exactly two months ago and up to this day he was camping out on the sofa. Had I been him I would have left her nagging ass in a heart beat! Didn't any hard working man like my father deserve to be treated how my mother was treating him. She had her way with everyone and being the spoil brat she was, she didn't know how to treat a soul. It was always all about her and if it wasn't about her it was a major problem. I guess that's where I developed some of my selfish ways from. "Woman I'm so tired of all of the nagging. I come home from work and expect a meal, maybe a back massage and some damn affection yet all I get is you bickering!" He grimaced. "You didn't give me anything to love nor want! What the hell did you expect!" My mother began yelling and I could hear things being tossed around downstairs. I climbed out of bed, I couldn't handle the verbal torture a second longer. I threw on a pair of jogging shorts and a tank top. I walked over to the window and started to climb out of it. Seeing a figure running across the back yard I noticed it was Tesa. "Tesa!" I yelled out the window. She stopped in her tracks and turned around. "What do you want Lisa?" She hollered back. "Wait for me." I told her. I closed the window back and eased down the steps my mother was so busy tearing up photos of her and my father from their memory book. My father caught me and our eyes locked. I raised my hand to my mouth and blew him an air kiss for leaving out of the backdoor. See my father and I had a bond like no other, only the two of us could understand. "Where are you going?" I met up with Tesa and questioned her. "Away from here. I can't deal with mommy and daddy fighting all day and all night. When is she going to just put his ass out so we can move on with life." Tesa replied. I stopped in my tracks, I couldn't believe her, for her to easily want my father out of her lives. He was her father after all, how could she not want him around still. "He's our father Tesa." I told her. She shrugged her shoulders, "Lisa I don't give two damns who he is. He's disgusting and I'm not claiming him as my father anymore. He won't embarrass me." Tesa explained.

"If he leaves who's going to pay the bills? You know mommy ain't going to lift a damn finger yet alone work a 9 to 5." I told her. Tesa shrugged her shoulders. "Well she better find something out. She'll probably just find some rich sucker to take care of her and us." Tesa replied. I shook my head at her. She was drop dead gorgeous but at times was as dumb as they came. Fooling with my mother rand believing everything my mother had told her she stayed with her head stuck up in the clouds living a fairytale life. We walked to the corner and Tesa's best friend Jasmine was parked in her Toyota Corolla waiting for us. Tesa jumped in the front seat and I got in the back. We wasn't even in the car for 3 seconds before Tesa started running all of our family's business in. "Girl we need to go get some smoke. I need to relax my mind. You just wouldn't believe the fuck shit that just happened today." Tesa started. I kicked her seat so hard her head went flying towards the dashboard. Jasmine, always in at the need of gossip quickly turned her music down. "What happened?" She asked as if she was really concerned. Tesa ran her fingers through her hair. "Everything happened. Let's go get something to smoke." Jasmine turned her music back up. "I thought you was about to drop some gossip on me!" She laughed. I stared at Jasmine. She was Tesa's best friend but I didn't like her for many reasons. For one she was sneaky, two she loved to gossip, three she was a shit started and the list went on and on. But Tesa loved that girl so much she would drink her dirty bath water! Jasmine was very gorgeous with a nice coke shape bottle body. And because of her flat stomach and nice round and plumped rear end you couldn't tell her a damn thing. She consider herself as a big body Benz. She was so full over herself it was sickening. She was high yellow but if you asked her she would easily lie and tell you that she was every race but african american, I guess all that fake Brazilian hair that she wore and the hazel contacts made her feel like she was otherwise. But underneath that weave displayed the nappy negro naps that one could have. Jasmine pulled up to Pennsylvania Ave, which was the weed, crack, dope and anything you want strip in West Baltimore. I pulled out my earbuds and placed them in my ear as she slowly drove down the street, checking out the scene and finding her weed boy. She pulled over in front of a skating rink and as soon as she rolled her window down our car was surrounded with a whole bunch of boys. Jasmine loved all the attention, she was floating and smiling from cheek to cheek. Her and Tesa was always boy happy, they both jumped out of the car. I sat in the car and listened to my music until I heard a knock at the door. I opened the door a bit and there was this guy standing there. He appeared to be a little bit older than me. "May I help you?" I asked. He flashed me a smiling showcasing his mouth full of gold teeth. "Can you help me?" He smiled. He opened the door a bit. "Slide over." He told me and climbed into the car. I looked him up and down, he was cute and he looked like he had a little bit of money. If I didn't learn anything from my mother one thing I learned to was never give a broke man any of my precious time. Because at the end of the day, bills didn't get paid off of love. "What do you do for a living?" I instantly asked him. "Damn, I'm still young. I'm just trying to live but meanwhile I'm out here getting this money. These streets are my 9 to 5." He told me. I nodded my head with approval. He didn't have to go in and punch anyones clock, as long as she was dedicated to some sort of hustle I was fine with that. "What's your name?" I asked. "Dough." He replied. "Dough because you are getting that dough huh?" I stated. We ended up chilling on Pennsylvania Ave for a few hours and the entire time Dough and I got to know one another. Suddenly Tesa and Jasmine walked over towards the car. The both of them have devilish grins on their faces. I knew the two of them was up to no good. Tesa snatched the door open that was closer to me and Jasmine snatched the other one open. "Your homeboy said for you to come here." Jasmine said to Dough. Dough looked at me. "I'll be right back." He told me and got out of the car. Tesa jumped in the car and started hitting me across my face. "Don't you dare think I forgot that you tried to kill me earlier!" She said. I pushed her off of me and started defending myself and hitting her back. Test was the type to actually show off we she had an audience, she was just like my mother. She loved the extra attention, rather it was good or bad. Jasmine came from behind me and wrapped her arms around my neck, Tesa grabbed me by my legs and pulled me out of the car. I could feel the both of them striking, they both were so weak for them to jump me. I kicked and screamed but couldn't get the two of them off of me for nothing! Finally Dough came rushing over towards us and broke us up. "Aren't ya'll sisters?" He questioned. "Why both of ya'll jumping her?" He questioned. I was too embarrassed. I got up from the ground and mugged the life out of both of them and got in the back seat of Jasmine's car. "Take me home right now!" I demanded. Tesa and Jasmine both got in the car and just like that we acted as if none of it never happen. Or so they think. Tesa nor Jasmine apologized to me or nor did they say a word to me. But that was cool, payback was a bitch and Tesa was an even worse bitch.

The entire time Dough and I talked I didn't think about the devastating situation that was going on back at home between my mother and my father all until we pulled out to our home and all the lights in the house were on. That's when reality sunk in. Good thing that I was high and a bit tipsy, nearly numb so none of the nonsense wasn't going to phase me. "Goodnight Jasmine!" I waived at her when Tesa and I got out the car. As she was pulling off I flipped her the bird. When Test and I walked in the house you would have thought a tornado had hit us. Furniture was flipped upside down. Broken glass was all over the floor, tables were flipped, the house was a complete mess. You could hear my mother and father upstairs still arguing and fighting.

Bouns

I went to my room, changed my clothing, just as I was climbing into bed my phone started to ring. I looked down at it and noticed that it was Dough calling me. Smiling from ear to ear I picked up the phone. "Hey." I softly cooed. "What are you doing?" He replied. I sat on the edge of my bed, "Nothing, I was just about to get in bed. Why what's up?" I questioned. I climbed fully into the bed and slid underneath the covers. "I was just thinking about you and how sexy you are." He explained. "Is that right?" I smiled. "Yeah Lisa, what do you have on?" He asked.

I looked at my PJ set that I had on with the Little Pony print all over them. I thought how childish it was me to still be wearing something of that sort. Dough was older so it was a must that I stepped my game up. "Nothing. I don't have anything on." I spoke. "Is that right." He said in a very seductive and soft voice. Him and I flirted a bit and he got straight to the point. "Slide your hands underneath the cover and put them between your thighs." He instructed. I got up and turned the lights off and did as he told me. I tuned my mother and father's arguing out and gave Dough all of my attention. I spread my legs and underneath the covers I slid my hands between my thighs. Dough instructed on what he wanted me to do and before I knew it he had me masturbating for the first time. I opened my legs a bit more as he instructed for me to put three fingers deep inside of me. I moved my fingers around and finally found some new excitement to my life. I was having sex and all of that but I really was doing it more for the fun then anything. Hell I found more joy in masturbating then actually having sex. "Is it wet?" Dough softly moaned. I shook my head, "Yes baby it's real wet." I moaned back. My fingers were so wet as I moved two of them inside of me and fingers my clitoris with my thumb. I grabbed ahold of my breast and started pinching my nipples with that hand. At that moment I wanted Dough in the worst way. "Move it faster. Come for daddy." He cooed. I did exactly what he told me, speeding up the pace I moved my little fingers faster and faster and went deeper and deeper inside of me. "Ohhhh-h-h Dough baby, I'm about to-" I began to announce. "Lisa!" I heard my father's voice. I was disrupted, humiliated and upset all at the same time. I jumped up and dropped the phone. "Daddy! What are you doing?" I asked. I pulled the covers up to my chest and could instantly feel my face blushing red. "I need to use your phone. Your mother broke my phone." My father said. "Oh." I embarrassedly dug for my cell phone underneath the covers. I purposely wiped the juices off my hands underneath the covers. Grabbing my cell phone I could still hear Dough going at it. I ended the call and handed my father the phone. He awkwardly looked at me but he didn't say anything to me. He knew he had to much other shit to deal with and not just that his baby girl was getting much older and things like so was bond to happen. He sat on the day bed that was next to my window. I took that opportunity to wrap myself out of the overs, grab some clothing and went into the bathroom to bathe and finished what my father interrupted. Dough had me hot as hell and I couldn't stop thinking about him. When I was done bathing, I stepped out of the tub, got dressed and walked towards my parents bedroom. My father was in the room with my mother, she was laying across the bed drinking out of a bottle of alcohol. Her eyes met with mines, her hair was disheveled and her make up was running all over the place. "He's not leaving, he's not going anywhere." She sniffled as black tears danced down her face. "He's going to love me." My mother assured me or more so tried to convince herself about something that she knew wasn't going to happen. I nodded my head. "Everything is going to be okay." I told my mother. I eased out of room and walked downstairs to see if my father was home. But he was nowhere to be found. I walked outside and checked the garage and noticed that his car was gone. I jotted back up stairs to see who he called off my phone. My mind was pondering and thoughts of him going to my God father's house crossed my mind but my father couldn't have been that much of a fool or maybe he was. I shook my head looking at Steven's number as the last call in my phone. I noticed three missed calls from Dough too. I turned the lights off, locked my bedroom door and called Dough back. Just as him and I engaged into a conversation I heard a loud bang at my door. "He left! I know he's with that man!" My mother screamed from the other side of the door. "I'll call you right back." I told Dough and ended the call. I couldn't wait until my birthday came around so I could turn eighteen and move into my own place where there was peace and quiet. My parents were driving me insane with all the banging on my door. I snatched the door open and my mother stood on the opposite end with Tesa standing next to her. "Daddy left. I bet he's at Steven's house! How can he leave us like this when our family is going through all of this madness." Tesa spoke. I stared her up and down and couldn't believe what was coming out of her mouth. Her and my mother standing there next to each other favored more as sisters than mother and daughter. Not to mention how the duo was just alike. "Get dress, we are going over to Steven's house." My mother told me. I stood there, I didn't have plans on going anywhere. I just wanted them to let my father be, yet they wanted to keep bullying him. I even heard my mother telling him to leave earlier that day and she had put all of his clothes out now she was chasing him. It was like she was cold then she was hot, very unpredictable and sure as hell damn hard to please. "I'm not going. I have school in the morning." I told the two of them. "I said put your damn clothes on Lisa!" My mother screamed on the top of her lungs like a mad woman. I jumped back and rushed towards my closet to grab a pair of sweat pants and a top. By the time I got dressed they were already in the kitchen rambling around. My mother grabbed a kitchen knife and so did Tesa. The thoughts of them doing any harm to my father made my heart ache. I loved him to death and I was going to let dumb and dumber do any more harm to him than we all had already done. I sat in the back seat of the car and text my God father's phone, giving him heads up I told him that we were on our way over there. Just as my mother predicted as we pulled up, my father's car was parked next to Steven's Dodge Ram. "Do you see this shit?" My mother asked us while breaking down crying. It had to hurt her for her man to leave her in the middle of the night to be with another man. I didn't know what my father was thinking. I didn't understand why he just couldn't chill out. "See he don't love us. He loves Steven more than us. If he loved us after we caught him doing what he did today he would have been at home trying to make things work. Not just with him and I but with his family too." She recited. And what my mother said really had me thinking. If my father truly loved us he would have been trying to make things work. Not go and get his ass waxed by our God father. My mother jumped out of the car with Tesa on her tail. I jumped in the driver seat as the two of them destroyed my father's car and Steven's car. They sliced three tires on each of their cars, broke a few windows and managed to scratch their cars up before Steven came running outside carrying some of foreign object in his hands. My mother and Tesa jumped in the car and being the getaway driver I pulled off in a hurriedly. "Be careful who you call in love with. Don't you two ever give a man your heart fully. You see what happens when you love someone and give them your all? They run all over top of you. Snatch your heart out of your chest and run with it." My mother started to school Tesa and I. Turning us both into hating men at a young age. "Fuck your father, he's going to pay for everything he did to us." My mother said. At that moment, I started to see things the way Tesa and my mother was seeing things and I hated to admit it. I loved my father but I was also starting to dislike him a bit. What was happening in our home was starting to do some things to me and had me in a slump of negativity.

Bouns

Being that Tesa and I was out all night with my mother being juvenile delinquents my mother didn't make us go to school the next day. When I woke up I could hear her and Tesa laughing and giggling. I climbed out of bed and went to my mother's room where the two of them were at. "Rise and shine sunshine." My mother cooed. I was elastic that she was in a better mood than the night before. "Good morning." I said to her and Tesa. Tesa was sitting in the indian position on my parents bed with my father's laptop sitting across her lap. "What are you guys doing?" I asked them. Both of them had devilish grins on their face and when the two of them were together I knew they were up to no good. Besides that with my mother smiling from ear to ear with everything going on I knew it had to be something that was benefiting her and hurting the next. She thrived off the next person's misery. "We logged into daddy's Sprint account and got ahold of all of his text messages and pictures that he's been sending Steven! And then we logged into his Google account and there's even more dirt in there!" Tesa announced with a burst of excitement. My mother beckoned me to come join them. At the time I didn't know she was forcing me into hating my father just like her and Tesa and not knowing I slowly fell into her little trick. "Come see what your father's been up to." My mother babbled. I was sort of perturbed but at the same time hesitant to see what they were looking at. "See look at these messages daddy had been sending Steven for months now!"

Tesa pointed out. She began reading the aloud. "Steven I never loved anyone like I love you. Steven please be patient with me, I'm going to be leaving them soon. I promise you love, that I work hard daily for you. I almost have enough money save up to move us far away were no one will no our name. I love you and when I love, I fight damn hard for the one I love." As Tesa read the messages I became sicker and sicker by the second. I looked back at my mother and tears escaped from her eyes. She licked her bottom dry lip. "I never in a million years thought your father would do this to us." She said emphasizing the 'Us'.

I closed my eyes and allowed the tears to escape my eyes too. My father really betrayed us and not once in any of his messages did I read him saying that he was going to do anything for us. Everything was about Steven. He had enough money saved up for him and Steven to go some place where no one knew who they were. So he was planning on leaving us. I see why my mother was so upset. My father was a coward and she had every right in being mad at him and even hating him. "What are we going to do?" I asked my mother. My mother shook her head. "Let's go take all of his money out of the bank!" Tesa finally came up with something brilliant. My mother's eyes lit up and she couldn't jump out of the bed any faster. I rushed in my room and got dressed too then rushed in the bathroom and brushed my teeth and ran a comb through my hair. An hour later we were pulling up to the SunTrust bank and as they say bad news circulated it came in threes and sometimes more. My father had two over drawn accounts with not a penny in them! "How much was withdrawn and when was it withdrawn?" My mother asked. Hearing that it was withdrawn five days prior my mother was beyond devastated. My father literally took all of his money and didn't leave us with a penny to survive on. My mother sat behind the steering wheel and bellowed a loud and ignorant scream. She broke down crying, she as shaking and yelling so bad I thought she was in the process of having a mental breakdown. Tesa and I both wrapped our arms around her and assured her that everything was going to be okay. But I wasn't too certain of that and either was Tesa. We both were young as hell at the age of Seventeen and Eighteen we just wanted our family back and to show our mother that everything was going to be okay. The drive back to the house was dreadful as we all thought about our future and how we were going to take care of home. When we got home we went to our room and my mother went to hers. I felt sorrow for her and felt her pain as I heard her loud cries escaping from her room. She was really hurting and it hurt just to see how terrible she was hurting. I decided to try and reach out to my father through my God father. I dialed his number and waited for Steven to pick up the phone. Without any luck they didn't answer the phone. So I then sent a text message. Excited to get a message back I opened up and read it. 'Please leave us alone.' The message read. Tears rolled down my cheeks as I read the words aloud. "Please leave us alone." How dare my father just abandon us the he was doing us. I couldn't think of anything that we done that was so horrible him to cause his reactions. I was willing to accept my father for who he was, regardless of what he did I wasn't going to hold that against him. We were all humans and humans were very unpredictable, so I didn't want to fault him at all. But seeing how he was starting to treat us, there was no way I could accept the things he did, especially when he didn't have any remorse for what he had did.

The hatred in my heart towards him started to grow thicker and thicker by the second. I laid in my bed and allowed the tears to flow from my eyes. I felt hopeless and lost, what were we going to do without my father who was the bread winner. I couldn't recall a time where my mother worked a 9 to 5 or when she did anything to actually put the food on the table or to keep a roof over our head. It was always about my father. The ringing of my phone caught my attention, I looked down at it and seen that it was Dough calling. "Hello. What are you doing?" I answered. "I was thinking about you. How is your day sweetheart?" He asked. I rolled over in bed and pulled the covers over my head. "Are you busy?" I asked him. "Nah, not yet." He replied.

"Good come see me." I told him. When he agreed, I hung up the phone and rushed to the shower. The slump that my mother was in she wasn't in no shape to come bother me and besides that she barely came to my room to check up on me. I jumped out the shower and rushed to clean my room up. I then lotion my body and sprayed some of my smell good on. By the time I got done Dough was texting me telling me he was outside. It was a piece of cake sneaking him inside. I laid two wet towels under the door and opened up my bedroom window as he rolled up a big fat blunt to help me cope with life. I looked over at him, he was so handsome. His short dreads was neatly twisted back into four braids, his arms were covered in tattoos, his clean face was as smooth as a baby's butt. He licked his lips and looked at me while he twisted the blunt. "You are so sexy." He told me. I smiled, "You are too." I replied. Thoughts of my mother telling Tesa and I to not fall for any dudes and not give our all ran across my mind. Thinking of how heart broken she was frightened me. I didn't ever want to be in her situation. Crying and depressed over a man who no longer wanted me or his children. I looked down at Dough's pocket and noticed the big lump in there. At that moment, I realized that nothing was for free and not just that. Who the hell was going to spoil me and buy me all of the newest clothing that I wanted and keep my hair and nails done since my father was no longer going to be around. Dough lit the tip of the blunt and looked at me and took a deep pull of the blunt. I laid in bed next to him and began to run my fingers through his hair. He took a few more pulls then passed it to me. I did the same and we continued that routine until the blunt was all gone. Sky high we laid next to each other. "Take your clothes off." He told me. I nodded my head and stood up and started to take my clothes off. "Dough, do you think you can help me with my phone bill?" I asked him. Nothing was free, I liked him but I truly didn't know how much he liked me and the last thing I wanted was to be taken advantage of. He helped me pull my shirt over my head and unsnap my bra. "How much is it?" He questioned. "Two hundred dollars." I replied in a jiffy. He nodded his head and pointed towards his pants that were laying on the floor. "Get it then." He instructed me. I picked up his pants and was filled with excitement as I pulled the money out of his pants and peeled off twelve twenties. I figured I would treat myself to a little extra money and with all the money he had he wouldn't have known the difference. I placed the money in my jewelry box, finished taking off rest of my clothing and climbed into the bed with him. He started kissing all over my body and licking me weirdly. It was a big turn off the way he licked me up and down like he was some sort of mutt yet I went with the flow. Finally he got to my hotbox and started to slowly lick it. The shit was so dry and boring I caught myself falling asleep on him twice. I couldn't believe what was happening. A few dreadful and dry moments later he came up and started kissing me all over my face. I swear he must have been a dog and I was his owner the way he was licking me. I was beyond disgusted, I wanted him to put it in already and carry his butt home. I was so bored! I closed my eyes and allowed him to kiss and lick all over my body and then suddenly I felt it entering me. "Oh Lord!" I opened my eyes, reaching between my thighs I felt his thick manhood and I thought after all I was going to be getting something out of the deal. He was so thick, hard and long I couldn't wrap my hands around it, I needed both of my hands to do so. He leaned down and started kissing me and finally I gave into him. "Ohhh Dough..." I pleasantly moaned as he took his time filling me up with his thickness. I grabbed the remote controller to my television and turned it up so I wouldn't get caught. I ran my hands across his back scratching the hell out of it. He continued to kiss me all over my face. I pushed him off of me, "Let me get on top." I told him. He laid flat on the bed with a grin painted on his face I climbed on top of him. I got on top of him and surprised the hell out of him as I rode him like a damn bull. "Ohhh. Yesss!" I moaned while squeezing my breast and puling on my nipples. He grabbed a hold of my waist and ran his hands all over my upper area. I looked up at the door and noticed that it was being opened. The stuff was so good there was no way I was going to stop until I exploded all over him. Tesa eyes met with mines as she held a butter knife in her hands, which she used to get in my room with. She covered her mouth and started giggling. I waived for her to exit the room instead she insisted on staying in the door frame giggling. So I ignored her and continued to get my groove on. "Ride it like you want it baby." Dough said encouraging me to go harder than I was already going. "I'm about to come." I told him so he could get prepared. Once I came all over him it was over with, so if he knew better he had better caught his while he could. He grabbed me by my hips and tossed me on the bed, pulling my legs back he pulled me to the very end up the bed. I bent over and moved back a tad bit further as he entered me from the back. He slapped me so hard across my butt that I fell on my stomach. I got back up and he did the same thing again. I knew my rear end probably was red as heck as hard as he slapped me. But nonetheless that rough stuff turned me on. He stuck his manhood inside of me and began pounding the life out of my insides. My legs started to shake, I looked up and Tesa was gone. I buried my head into the pillows and sensationally cried tears of pleasure. "Uhhhh." He grunted and collapsed right beside me. I climbed up to my pillows and got underneath the covers and cuddled up. Shorty after I was drifting off to sleep.

Bouns

Later that day I woke up and Dough was gone, I looked over on my dresser and noticed a bag filled with weed and noticed a few twenty dollar bills laying next to it. I picked the money up and counted it, he had left me an extra two hundred dollars on top of the two hundred dollars that he had already given me. I took the money and placed it in my hiding spot in the closet. I then text him and told him to bring his butt back over later that night. I walked out of my room and jotted down the steps and noticed that my mother still haven't cleaned the mess up that her and my father had made. Which I knew she wasn't going to because she was as lazy as they came. It wasn't my mess and it wasn't going to get cleaned by me either. So I stepped right over everything and made my way to the kitchen to make me something to eat. Walking back upstairs I heard my mother fussing on the phone. "Steven you ruined my family!" She cried over the phone. I stood at her door listening to her and my God father argue back and forth. My mother took her cell phone and tossed it across the room. "I just want my family back." She cried out. I peeped in her and noticed that she was drinking. Before my father and my mother's break up my mother barely took a drink now that him and her was going through their break up all she did was lay in bed and drink her life away. "I'm going to go to his job. He wants to hang up on me. I got something for him." My mother said to herself and started to get dress. I rushed past her room to mines and sat my food on the dresser then rushed to the bathroom to take a quick shower by the time I got done my mother was walking out of her room. "Wait mommy, can I come with you?" I asked her. I was a bit angry at my father too, my mother no longer had to fight the battle that her and my father had alone. It was now our battle. My mother pulled up to my father's job twenty minutes later and as we were pulling up Steven was pulling off so quick he didn't even notice us pulling in. "What are we going to do?" I asked my mother. A big smile came across her face. "I want to humiliate him. He left us without anything and I want him to be left without anything too." My mother said backing out of her parking spot. So instead of going into the law firm that he worked in, we sat outside and waited across the street for him to get off. Which was two hours later. Steven pulled up and my father came walking outside and got in the car with Steven. My mother and I trailed a bit behind them, their first stop was down on Pulaski Highway at the Longhorn. Steven got out of the truck and went and opened my father's door for him like he was the man of the relationship and my father was the women. The entire time my mother had her phone out recording everything. Even when they were sitting down eating and I swear I never seen my father smile the way Steven had him smiling from ear to ear. My mother made sure anything that could humiliate my father she had it on recording. At the end of their little dinner when they walked outside and shared a long passionate kiss it brought tears to my eyes. I looked over at my mother and she was crying too. I held her hand, "I love you mommy." I told her trying to lighten up the situation a bit. But I know that did nothing. She was hurt and angry and was probably still had questioning lingering around in her mind that my father prohibited to answer them. Leaving her without answers turned her into a mess, it was un fair for the way he did our family and he was going to pay for it by all means. "I want to hurt him so bad. I want him to feel exactly how I feel. I want him to cry every damn night. I want him to know that he's being punished for what he have done to us." My mother said in a raged tone on our way back home. I nodded my head agreeing with her. When we pulled up to the house ideas started to come to my mind. Steven and my father was going to pay for everything they did. "Do Steven work tonight?" I asked my mother. My mother scrunched her face up and thought for a second. "Yes he does." She replied. I nodded my head and climbed out of the car. When I got inside the house the entire house smelled like weed. We walked into the house and Tesa and Jasmine was sitting on the couch, smoking and chilling as if they weren't inside of my parents home. Any other time Tesa knew the shit she was doing wouldn't have happened. But I guess she figured since my mother was down and out she would try her and do what she want. My mother started sniffing like a greyhound as she as she stepped foot in the house. Tesa jumped up and greeted us with a dry "Hey." My mother threw her bag on the stand that rested beside the door. "Is that weed you are smoking in my house." She asked Tesa as if she didn't already recognize the strong smell. Tesa nodded her head. I swear she had to be to darn high because she was acting so stupid. "Yes it is." She replied back to my mother. Never in my life had I seen Tesa be so disrespectful with my mother but my mother should have known that this day was going to come soon or later. My mother drew her hand back and slapped the hell out of Tesa. "Who the hell do you think you are? Tesa grabbed her face and burst out crying. She was such a spoil brat, she wasn't use to my mother nor my father discipling her. My mother grabbed the weed off the table and when she did I noticed what type of bag it was in. I instantly thought about the weed that Dough had given me. I was thinking to myself if Tesa had stolen my weed I was going to beat the breaks off of her butt. While her and my mother argued back and forth I walked upstairs to check my stash, thankful it was still there. I walked back down the steps and Tesa and my mother was still arguing, I sat back and kind of enjoyed the two of them going at it. Maybe Tesa wasn't going to be the golden child for too long. My mother stuffed Tesa's weed in her purse. "All you going to do is smoke it yourself. Since daddy's have been gone you been turning into a complete stranger." Tesa hissed and folded her arms around her chest. My mother smiled, "Since your father left I been able to find myself as a person. I'm no longer being controlled. I'm almost happy and I'm sure as heck is free now! And you are so right Tesa, I just may roll up me a little joint and free my mind." My mother tried to convince herself but we all knew otherwise. She was as miserable as miserable came.

Tesa stood up and grabbed her purse from off the table. "I'm going out." She announced. My mother stared her up and down. "You are getting too damn grown for your own good. I think it's about time you start apartment searching after graduation. This house isn't big for two women." My mother announced. Tesa nodded her head agreeing, "I think I might just do that." She said walking to the door. Jasmine smiled and waived to my mother. "Hi Mrs. Nancy, I'm so sorry what happened with your husband." Jasmine said and the two of them walked out of the door. I swear I didn't like Jasmine at all. I ran out behind them. "Can I come?" I asked Tesa. She shrugged her shoulders, I jumped in the back seat. "I can't believe your father like boys." Jasmine said starting the car up. Tesa started fidgeting with the music and turned in up. "Where are we going?" I asked. Jasmine turned around. "Should you have asked that before jumping in the car?" Jasmine replied. I shrugged my shoulders. I really didn't care where we were going. As long as I was out of the house I was good with that. We ended up pulling up on Mosher to Jasmine's boyfriend Pernell's house. Pernell was this cute and tall guy, with these crazy light brown eyes and deep dimples. Way too cute for Jasmine, however him and her had been going together for over two years. He played basketball, did a little hustling on the side and with those two things alone Jasmine swore up and down that he was going to go pro and get her out the hood some day. That's the mean reason why she treated him like a golden token, she just knew he was her meal ticket.

When we pulled up on his block, his porch was crowded with guys as always. I barely got to go to his house because Jasmine and Tesa never wanted me to hang out with them. Jasmine parallel parked her car and threw it in park. We opened our doors and got out the car. Walking up to Pernell's step I noticed his homeboys with uneasy looks on their faces. Then I spotted two females sitting on his swing porch. When they seen us they instantly started looking guilty about something. "What's up? Where's Pernell's big head ass at?" Jasmine spoke. None of his boys wanted to answer her for some reason. Whatever the case was they all looked guilty as hell. Test looked over at the two girls who were sitting on the swing. "Hi." She cooed. Jasmine looked at his boys, "What y'all ain't speaking today?" She questioned. She then reached for the door handle and walked in the house. I sat down on the step and Tesa grabbed a seat in between the girls on the swing. Seconds later we heard a lot of yelling and screaming. Tesa jumped up and ran inside of the house, out of nowhere a girl came running out screaming and yelling wearing nothing but her birthday suit. Tesa and Jasmine came running out behind her. Tesa pushed the girl off the porch, she fell right on her face. She let out a loud scream and tried to get up and run but Tesa and Jasmine was too quick for her. Jumping on top of the girl beating her violently. "You thought you wasn't going to get caught messing with my man?" Jasmine yelled while stomping the girl face. Her friends stood up but didn't dare to do a damn thing, in fact they looked so damn scared they started to ease off the porch not once did they try to help their friend. Pernell came to the door frame wearing nothing but his birthday suit too. His eyes met with mines and they followed me all the way down to his manhood. When he seen what I was looking at he quickly attempted to cover it up with his hands but there was no use for him to do that. The thing he was toting there was no way he was going to hide it by covering his hands. He turned around and rushed back into the house. Jasmine and Tesa was still beating the breaks off the girls. Pernell came back out now with clothes on and attempted to break up the fight by grabbing Jasmine off the girl. Blood was everywhere, "Get off me Pernell. How dare you do me like this?" Jasmine cried. I stood back on the porch and watched the chaos, it was actually kind of funny to watch. Jasmine was always popping her gums and stayed in everyone's business. Now she finally had some sort of drama to deal with herself. Jasmine started swinging on Pernell, hitting him all in the face. He kept ducking and dodging her hits. His homeboys were all now standing up and looking at all the drama. The girl crawled over to her friends and they helped her to the ground and they helped her into a grey car. Jasmine slapped Pernell so hard across his face he lost his balance and fell onto the ground. She ran up to him and started kicking him all in the stomach and the face. He caught one of her kicks and pulled her down, causing her to fall on her face. "Ahhh." Jasmine screamed. Jumping to her feet she held her mouth, blood was gushing from out of her hands. She looked down at the blood and started screaming even louder. Jasmine rushed to her car, "I can't believe you did this to me Pernell!" She hollered with blood dripping from her mouth while jumping in the driver seat. Tesa ran behind her and got in the car. I stepped off the porch and rushed to the car. When I got to the back door I realized it was lock. Jasmine rolled down the back window. "You stood there the entire time and didn't help me, so I ain't helping you with a ride!" Jasmine yelled at me and quickly pulled off into the street. I was so confused to what had happened. But Jasmine made a big mistake for leaving me that day. She was as cruel as they came. How dare did she leave me after she knew that her and Tesa had jumped a female and they could retaliate and come back for me. Secondly why would I jump into a fight when her and Tesa was doing just fine beating the breaks off the girl. Embarrassed I turned around to face Pernell and his boys. "Let me use your bathroom." I said to Pernell. "Go ahead." He told me. In his bathroom I sat on the toilet and thought about the long walk back home. I was going to call my mother but I decided not to bother her after everything she was already going through. I then started blowing up both Tesa and Jasmine's phone but both of them ignored my call....

FOR MORE OF this book "Hoeism and Matrimony" order www.iamangelwilliams.com

. . .

Star City Publications Books
www.starcitypublications.com
www.IamAngelWilliams.com

ALSO BY ANGEL WILLIAMS

WE SHIP TO PRISONS! MAIL US FOR A CATALOG

PO BOX 7322 HARRISBURG PA 17113

Envy The Root Of All Evil 1

Envy The Root Of All Evil 2

Envy The Root Of All Evil 3

Envy The Root Of All Evil 4

Pretty Money

Gold Diggin Honeys

Momma I Ain't No Saint

Raven's Cravings Book

Raven's Cravings movie

The Bentleys

The Perfect Side Nigga

Hell Between My Thighs

FOU

Love On LockDown

Ryder: Every Thug Needs A Ryder

Untamed & Deranged Mates

Sweet Lyric

The Streets Can Wait But My Love Won't

Almighty Dollar

Hell In My Life...Real Rap

Hell In My Life...Real Rap 2

Hell In My Life...Real Rap 3

Could It Be Love 1

Could It Be Love 2

Could It Be Love 3

Could It Be Love 4 (Coming Soon)

BedRoom Boom

Rhonda's Lesson

The Mercedes Story Book 1

Wife Swap

Hoeism & Matrimony 1

Hoeism & Matrimony 2 (Coming Soon)

Passion, Pain & Pleasure

There's No Love In The Trenches

Low Down & Dirty Lovers 1

Low Down & Dirty Lovers 2

You Gon Luv Me

Married N Sluttin It (Coming Soon)

Sweet Lyric 2 (Coming Soon)

So Damn Juicy 1 -10

****

To Order Books Send Money Order To Po BOX ANGEL WILLIAMS 7000 GOLDEN RING RD, UNIT 70384 ROSEDALE MARYLAND 21237 With taxes & Shipping books are $15.88 Per book

Order Form

Title:

Title:

Title:

Title:

Title:

Title:

Shipping Address:

If Inmate please include inmate ID # & any special shipping information

Made in the USA
Las Vegas, NV
23 October 2023

79596838R00100